Cottage at Gooseberry Bay:
Thanksgiving Past

by

Kathi Daley

②

Chapter 1

The house, which had most likely been loved and cared for by the family who'd lived there at one time, had been abandoned long ago. While the structure was shabby and faded, there was evidence that children had once played in the overgrown yard. A bicycle leaned against the peeling siding, a rope swing hung from a large tree, and a little pink bucket, faded from the sun, laid at the foot of a large shrub, which had been left to spread out unattended. I felt a moment of sympathy for the neglected home with its shuttered windows, cracked walkway, and lawn ravaged by weeds. According to the story I'd been told the previous evening, the family who'd been living in the two-story home with gingerbread trim had disappeared without a trace.

Without a trace. I rolled the concept around in my mind. How exactly does one disappear without a trace? The man, woman, and four children who'd once lived in the now dilapidated house had to be somewhere. Unless, of course, the family was dead and buried in an out-of-the-way place, which was an option too gruesome to consider, although, in the case of this particular family, it seemed as good an explanation as any. When my new friend, Parker Peterson, had told me the story of the missing family over dinner last night, I'd been intrigued, but as I stared at the little pink bucket and tried to imagine the child who'd once played with it, all I could feel was deep and penetrating sorrow.

"Ainsley, what are you doing all the way over on this side of town?"

I turned and looked at the dark-haired woman who'd walked up behind me. "Hope." I smiled at Hope Masterson, the owner of the local inn who'd started off as a landlord but had become a friend. "I didn't hear you approach."

"I was in the area visiting a friend who's been ill and was on my way back to the inn. I saw you standing here staring at the old Hamish place, so I thought I'd come over and say hi. You look sad. Are you okay?"

"I'm fine," I assured her. "I was just wondering about the family who once lived here."

"So, you've heard the story?"

I nodded. "Parker was hanging out at Josie and Jemma's place last night, and she filled me in. I guess

I was curious, so I decided to stop by." I gazed at the boarded up front door beyond the rotting front porch.

"The story of the Hamish family is quite the mystery," Hope responded. "The fact that the family was clearly preparing to sit down to dinner when they disappeared makes it even creepier in my mind. I guess Parker told you that the Thanksgiving turkey was still sitting on the kitchen counter waiting to be carved when the neighbor stopped by the following day."

I nodded. "Parker mentioned that fact and said it looked as if the family had just vanished into thin air. None of the neighbors claimed to have seen or heard a thing. There hadn't been any sign of forced entry or a struggle, and the family's personal possessions, including the family car, were left behind."

"It is a very odd mystery," Hope agreed. "And it's so disturbing. I don't know everything that happened, but I remember Parker diving into the deep end with that story. She was just getting started as a journalist, and I guess she realized that such an interesting story could provide her with her big break. She was frantic to solve the mystery and figure out what exactly happened to the Hamish family, but, like the cops, she never could figure it out."

"I think she intends to try again."

Hope raised a brow. "Really? After all this time? Does she have a new lead?"

"I don't think so. I think she just hopes that if she looks at the same leads that she had back then, they might make more sense after five years."

Hope leaned a hip against the short fence that bordered the front of the home. She paused as if taking a moment to organize her thoughts before she spoke. "I remember there were a lot of theories floating around at the time, which I suppose was natural since no one had any answers, and everyone was scared there was a serial killer in town and their family might be next to go missing. There were a few good theories put out there that could never be proven, but the reality is that most of the stories being circulated were nonsense."

"Such as?" I asked.

"I suppose the *out of the box* theory that gained the most attention five years ago was the alien abduction theory. Apparently, a handful of people had seen bright lights in the sky that night, and once word of the lights got out, there was a group who insisted that aliens had visited us. Of course, I didn't believe it for a minute, but I suppose that an alien abduction is about as believable as the claim that the mob abducted the family."

"Abducted by the mob? What mob?"

Hope shrugged. "I don't think anyone had a specific mob in mind. A family who disappears as they're getting ready to sit down for a meal just felt like a mob sort of thing to a lot of people."

"Yeah, I guess it does at that. What do you think happened?"

She glanced toward the house and then answered. "I really have no idea. I hope the family left of their own free will, but if they had, why not take a few things with them?"

"An abduction does make sense," I agreed. "Although I can also imagine a scenario where a family in hiding finds out that the person or persons who seek to harm them have found them and are on their way to the house, and the family leaves without even stopping to grab their personal possessions."

"Of course, if that had occurred, it seems as if the people who were after them would have shown up shortly after their departure only to find the house empty."

"That's true. If there had been someone after the family, they wouldn't have just knocked on the door and then left when no one answered. They would have broken in and taken a look around."

"Exactly. And if that would have occurred, it seems that someone, a neighbor perhaps, would have noticed that someone other than the family who lived in the house was on the property and called the police. Although..." Hope paused before continuing. "If you stop to think about it, a family on the run from an unknown threat is a good theory if you consider this specific town. Gooseberry Bay really is the perfect town to settle in if you want to get lost. Not only are we a small, close-knit community, but based on the geography created by the bays and inlets in the area, we're pretty isolated as well."

I pulled my sweater tighter across my body as a gust of wind blew through the neighborhood, sending the leaves that had littered the yards and streets flying. "That's a good point as well. I noticed that once you turn off the main road at the bridge, it's still another thirty miles south to town, and once the road reaches the town, it ends. It's not like you deal with a lot of folks just passing through on their way to somewhere else."

"Exactly," Hope agreed, tucking a stray lock of her dark hair behind her ear. "Which is why your theory of a family on the run seems to have merit. I think if you look hard enough, you'll find quite a few locals who seem to be harboring a secret."

I paused to think about that. I had to wonder if the woman I'd come here to find had been harboring a secret, which, like the secret I suspected the Hamish family had kept, had also caused her to run.

"Did you know the family?" I asked after a moment.

Hope picked up a bright red leaf that had settled onto her shoulder once the gust had passed. She twisted the stem mindlessly between her forefinger and thumb as she answered. "I knew them casually, although they weren't really the sort to establish close friendships. Mark, who I would say was close to forty, worked as a laborer for a local contractor. I'm not certain that I ever spoke to him since he wasn't the sort to socialize after work, but I remember seeing him around town from time to time. His wife, Mary, who I would guess might have been a few years younger, waited tables at a diner on the highway."

"Diner?" I asked.

"It was really just a hamburger joint called Jack's Place. It burned down a few years ago. Arson, I think. To be honest, it looked to be a bit of a greasy spoon, and I never ate there, but I remember noticing it as I drove in and out of the area. It tended to attract tourists passing by on their way into Gooseberry Bay."

Personally, I loved good greasy hamburgers. It was too bad it was gone. Those sorts of places usually had the best milkshakes. "So tell me more about the family."

"As I've already indicated, I didn't know them well," Hope answered. "I remember they had four children. All girls. The oldest was sixteen or seventeen, I guess. I remember that she attended the local high school. There were two girls between the oldest and youngest. I guess they might have been in elementary or even middle school. I seem to remember that the youngest was probably around five or six." Her smile faded. "Cute kids. Dark hair, big brown eyes, and petite features." She let out a shallow breath. "I thought about those four kids for the longest time after they went missing. I prayed every night that they were safely tucked away somewhere."

I looked at the house, which still stood empty after five years. "Did the Hamish family have relatives in the area?"

"Not that I know of. I suppose you can check with the neighbors, but I'm fairly certain that no one showed up looking for answers once the family disappeared. I remember there was an article in the newspaper asking folks to call the sheriff's office if they had any information that could lead to an explanation as to what happened to the family. The article also asked anyone who might know of any sort of next of kin to come forward, but as far as I know, no one did."

I looked at the old house that had caused me to pull over and park in the first place. "I suppose it's possible the Hamishs didn't have family, but it seems as if someone would have done something about the house by this point. There must be procedures in place to deal with a property if the owner dies, and no one comes forward to claim it."

"I suppose there might be, but I also suppose that if next of kin can't be established, what comes next is probably a complicated process. I guess if you're really interested, you can ask Deputy Todd about it."

I supposed Deputy Todd might know the status of the estate, but I also supposed that it really wasn't all that important. "Do you know how long the Hamish family lived here?"

"About two years. Maybe less." Hope brushed her hair away from her face. "I'm not exactly sure when they moved here, and I really have no idea where they came from, but I remember chatting with the oldest girl, Hannah, during our annual Christmas event the year before they disappeared, and she mentioned that she'd never experienced a white Christmas and had been hoping for one. I asked her where she'd lived before moving to Gooseberry Bay, and she simply said down south where it was hot over the holidays."

"I suppose Deputy Todd must have traced the family back to wherever they came from. I'll have to ask Parker. When we spoke, she indicated that she had notes and stuff. Even if she was just starting out, I bet she figured out the basics."

"Probably. Parker is a smart woman. She has a knack for finding what she needs to close the story she's after. If she'd had a bit more experience when the Hamish family went missing, I have no doubt she would have found closure for that story as well."

"Well, she seems determined to do just that now. Parker, Jemma, Josie, and I are all getting together tonight to come up with a game plan. I'm not sure we'll figure anything out that wasn't figured out five years ago, but Parker should have a story either way. If you want to help out, I'm sure you'd be welcome."

"I appreciate that, but it's a busy season at the inn, and I have the Christmas Village to plan and find volunteers for, so I think I'll pass."

"If you need volunteers, I'd be happy to help out," I offered.

She smiled. "Wonderful. There's a meeting Tuesday. I'll email you the specifics. Gooseberry Bay's Christmas Village is a huge event, and we really can use all the help we can get."

"I'm really looking forward to the holidays this year. The peninsula gang makes it seem as if a Gooseberry Bay Christmas is a magical experience." I referred to the three women and two men who lived on the same peninsula as I did at the north edge of Gooseberry Bay.

Hope smiled. "Oh, it is. People come from all around. If we have snow, it will be even better."

"I can imagine. Booker told me all about the boat parade, and Josie went on and on about all the colorful lights that folks put up all over town. Jemma seemed to be most excited about the huge decorated tree in the gazebo as well as the tree on the boardwalk, and Tegan made mention of a large variety of food vendors."

"Like I said, it's a huge undertaking, but it really does mean so much to almost everyone who lives in the area."

"Well, I, for one, can't wait."

Hope turned so that she was facing me directly rather than looking toward the house. "It seems as if you're fitting right in with the peninsula gang."

"I am," I confirmed. "Thank you again for renting to me. It's worked out perfectly so far. I love the coziness of the cottage, and I cherish the friends I've made. And of course, the dogs love having so much room to wander around."

Hope looked back toward my SUV. "Where are the dogs?"

"I took Kai and Kallie for a long run this morning, so I left them home to rest while I did some errands. They needed a nap, and I needed to run by the hardware store and the general store, and I didn't want to leave them in the car while I was inside. By the way, I wanted to let you know that I've finished painting the walls we talked about. You should stop by the cottage and have a look. You won't recognize the place."

"I'll do that. I'm anxious to see how it all worked out."

"The light bluish-gray was a good choice. It gives the cottage a very natural feel. I thought I might work on the walls in the attic room your uncle used for a studio over the winter. The room is just so awesome with all those windows, but so far, I'm not really using the space."

"It might make a good office for you if you're going to be around long enough to make it worthwhile setting one up."

"Actually, I do plan to stick around for a while — through the winter for sure and maybe even longer." I smiled. "I guess I'll have to see how everything works out, but I really love it here. I may even decide to settle here permanently once I get the answers I came looking for."

Hope smiled. "I spoke to Archie." She referred Archie Winchester, one of the two brothers who lived in the house I'd come to Gooseberry Bay to research. "He told me you were out at the house, and he said it appeared that you had been there before — when you were younger."

I nodded. "It did seem that way. When Archie first showed me the house, I wasn't entirely certain. The house in my dreams has presented itself to me in tiny fragments that don't necessarily fit together in any sort of organized manner. And the house Archie lives in is just so…" I struggled for the right word.

"Grandiose."

"Sort of, but in a good way. It is huge and very intimidating, but it's also extremely impressive. I loved the conservatory, and Josie told me that the ballroom is fabulous. I suppose the overuse of crystal chandeliers and ornamental trim did seem a bit ostentatious, but the view was spectacular, and the more I looked around, the more certain I was that I'd visited the house at some point. Archie didn't know who the woman in the photo was, but I'm hoping Adam will."

"Archie told me that Adam was in town while he was in London, but I wasn't aware of that fact, or I would have introduced you. He's a hard man to nail down."

"So I've heard. Based on what the others have said, he works a lot."

She nodded. "He really does, but he spends six or seven weeks from around mid-November through New Year's Day here every year, so he should be showing up in the next week or so, and then he'll be around for a while." She glanced back toward the house we were still standing in front of. "I'm not sure if Parker is going to end up with the answers she's after, but I really hope you get yours. It must be so odd not knowing how you ended up in the middle of a burning building on Christmas Eve when it appears that you were here at the house on Piney Point just months beforehand."

"I will admit that the whole thing has caused me some grief."

Hope glanced at her watch. "I should get going. I have a lot to do before check-in time."

"I imagine Fridays are your busiest day."

"They are." She pulled her phone out and sent a quick text. "Good luck with your meeting tonight. I hope you find something new to give your investigation some steam, but if you don't, I think I should warn you that Parker tends to go just a tiny bit crazy when a story isn't coming together."

"Good to know. Thanks for the warning."

After Hope returned to her car and continued on her way, I decided to take a walk around the property. I wanted to get a feel for things, so I would be able to visualize what Parker referred to when we met that evening. The house was situated on a large lot on a quiet street. There were homes on either side of the property, but they were set in the center of their own large lots, so the three structures weren't really all that close together. The backyard was fenced, but the gate was easy enough to open, so I popped the latch and headed around to the rear of the property. The grass was dead and overrun with weeds, the same as the grass in the front of the property had been. The upstairs windows were covered with shutters, as were the windows at the front of the house, but the downstairs windows were covered with large pieces of plywood. Small pieces of glass on the ground seemed to indicate that someone had broken the windows at the back of the house at some point, and whoever was supposed to be keeping an eye on the place had covered the openings with wood rather than replacing them.

There was a tall wooden fence around the entire property at the back. A small wooden gate along the back fence line provided access to the meadow behind the property. Beyond the meadow was a road, and on the other side of the road was a heavily forested hillside. I supposed if it had been dark when the family left their property, they could have snuck out the back and met up with a car that was waiting for them on the road behind the home, and no one, not even the neighbors on either side of the house, would necessarily have seen them.

I wasn't sure where the road that ran behind the home led, but if I had to guess, it probably hugged the hillside and then eventually met up with the main highway that ran along the bay. The bay road was the only road in or out of the area, so if the family had fled in a vehicle, they would have had to have taken that route which led to the bridge that crossed the inlet separating Gooseberry Bay from the road leading to Port Angeles.

I wondered what was on the other side of the wooded hillside. I'd need to look at a map. If the family had fled at the last minute as their enemy approached, they wouldn't have had time to arrange for a car and would have been on foot. In that case, it would have been safest to disappear into the woods rather than traveling along the highway. I felt a chill climb up my spine. I couldn't imagine the terror the family must have felt if they had been forced to run for their lives with only the clothes on their backs on what had most likely been a chilly night.

After I checked out the area behind the property, I headed back through the gate to the fenced yard. I took another walk around the house and then headed toward my SUV.

"Afternoon," a woman with long blond hair who looked to be in her early twenties approached from across the street. She was holding the hand of a child who looked to be around three.

"Afternoon," I replied.

"I noticed you were checking out the Hamish place," she said. "I live in the area and try to keep an eye on the place. Was there something you needed?"

"My name is Ainsley Holloway," I said. "I'm working with Parker Peterson, who works for the local newspaper. Parker is doing a follow-up story on the family who disappeared, and I was just here to take a look before our strategy meeting."

"I know who Parker is," the woman said. She held out a hand. "I'm Vanessa Hudson."

"Happy to meet you." I looked down at the child who was still clinging to the woman's hand. "And what is your name?"

"Arial."

"I'm happy to meet you, Arial." I really hadn't spent much time around children. Being an only child, I hadn't had nieces and nephews to dote on, nor did I have friends with children, but this little pixie sure was a cutie. I looked back toward the woman, whom I assumed was the girl's mother. "Did you live here when the family went missing?"

She nodded. "I moved to the area about the same time as the Hamish family. I was devastated when the family simply disappeared."

"I can imagine. I recently moved to the area, but based on what I've been told, the whole thing is quite the mystery." I smiled at Arial, who had walked over and sat down on the edge of the raised sidewalk. She scooped up a pile of brightly colored leaves and began stacking them neatly. "Did any of the family members say anything in the days or weeks before the incident that might explain what happened?"

"No. Not really." Vanessa furrowed her brow. "How exactly do you know Parker Peterson?"

"As I indicated, I recently arrived in Gooseberry Bay. I'm currently renting a cottage out on the peninsula. I became friends with the other residents who live out there, and Parker is a frequent visitor."

"I see."

"Do you know Parker well?" I asked.

"No. I've never even spoken to her in person, but I know who she is. I've read her articles, and I remember her covering the missing family for her newspaper at the time of the disappearance. I guess you can say I'm more of a fan than a friend."

"She's very talented," I agreed. "I guess you must be around the same age as the oldest Hamish girl, Hannah."

"Yes. We were in the same class in high school."

"I don't suppose you've heard from her since the family disappeared."

The woman hesitated before responding. I could see that she was trying to work something through in her mind. Her smile faded, and her previously open facial expression shuttered, as she seemed to have come to some sort of decision. "No, I haven't heard from Hannah. I'm pretty sure she's dead. I'm pretty sure they all are."

"You don't think they might have simply left the area for some reason?"

She shook her head. "I don't see why they'd just leave. I remember that Hannah really liked it here. I also remember her mentioning that the others liked it here as well." Her smile returned, although a distant look came across her face as she seemed to be remembering the family she'd once known. "Courtney was in the eighth grade when they lived here. She was the most outgoing of the sisters. The loudest as well. She was going through a rebellious phase during her time in Gooseberry Bay, and it seemed that she found herself in trouble more often than not. Still, I remember noticing how smart she was and how confident."

"Thirteen is a tough age," I agreed.

"It really is, but Courtney had gumption. She knew what she wanted, and she knew how to get it. I remember thinking that when she got older, she was going to rule the world. And anyone who knew her knew that she was going to do it on her own terms." Vanessa wiped a tear from her eye. "I hate the thought that she might never have had the chance to grow up."

"Yeah," I said. "It's such a tragic situation. Did you know the younger girls?"

She nodded. "Sarah was only ten and already into a lot of different hobbies. Mama wouldn't let her do any organized after-school activities, like ballet or gymnastics, but Sarah loved to draw, and she loved to read."

"Mama?" I asked.

"Her mama, Mary."

I nodded. "Go on."

"Laura was the baby of the family. She was six and had just started the first grade. She still liked to play with her dolls, and she was forever out in the yard burying things with her little pink shovel and bucket."

"Burying things? What sort of things?" I asked.

"Anything she could find." Her grin widened. "One time, she buried her daddy's car keys, and no one could find them. There was this huge search for them before Laura was finally convinced to give them up or lose her bucket and shovel forever."

"It sounds as if you knew the family well," I said.

She shrugged. "Yeah, I guess."

"You said you lived in the area at the time of their disappearance. Do you remember seeing anything at all on that Thanksgiving Day that might explain what happened?"

She hesitated before continuing. "No. I didn't see anything." She looked toward the house and then back at me. "But one of the other neighbors told me that they remembered seeing a car in the area."

"Car?"

"It was a blue, four-door sedan. I'm not sure of the make or model, but the neighbor said that it had been parked on the street in front of the Hamish home a few times in the days before the family disappeared. I don't suppose you've heard anything about the car."

"No. I just started working with Parker. I'll have to ask her about it. Do you remember anything else about the sedan?"

"I didn't notice the vehicle personally, but the neighbor I spoke to at the time told me that the windows were tinted, so it was hard to see inside. It was the opinion of this neighbor that there was someone sitting in the vehicle, watching the Hamish house."

"Does this neighbor still live in the area?" I wondered.

"No, he's long gone. It's too bad you can't talk to him about it. I kept thinking that the blue sedan might turn out to be the lead that would help the police find the family, but after that first bit of local gossip, I never heard another thing about it. Of course, I was just a kid. Well, maybe not a kid, but not an adult, either. Still," she added, "I have wondered about the investigation. I've wondered about what the police might have found. I've wondered if anyone ever identified the owner of the blue sedan."

"I'll have to ask Parker. I suppose she might know." I turned and looked back toward the house. "And you don't remember personally seeing the car?"

She shook her head. "No. I don't think so. But the man I spoke to said it was an average looking blue sedan. It wasn't the sort of car one would necessarily notice if it happened to drive by or park on the street."

I supposed that made sense. I can't say that I noticed the cars that parked on the street where I'd lived before moving to Gooseberry Bay. Still, the blue sedan seemed like a clue, given the timing. Part of me wanted to pay a visit to Deputy Todd to see if I could use my power of persuasion to get him to tell me what he knew, but I doubted he'd share anything of real value, and I supposed I should head home and get ready for dinner.

Arial had gotten up from the curb she'd been sitting on and walked over to her mother. I guessed she'd grown tired of stacking the leaves.

"I guess Arial and I should get home," Vanessa said.

"It was nice meeting you both." I smiled at the little girl and then looked up at the mother. "If I give you my phone number, would you be willing to call me if you think of anything else that might lead us to the answers we're after?"

"Sure, I can do that." She pulled her phone out of her pocket. I rattled off my digits, and she punched them into her phone. She slipped her phone back into her pocket without offering me her number in return.

I said goodbye to both Vanessa and Arial and watched as they walked away. I took one last look at the house and then climbed into my SUV. As I drove toward the peninsula, I forced my mind onto other topics. I thought about all the projects I still wanted to tackle to make the little cottage I'd rented feel like home, and I thought about the pilgrimage that had brought me to Gooseberry Bay. I thought about the cop who'd raised me, and the dreams I'd been having since his death. I thought about the photo of the woman on the porch of the house on Piney Point with two small children, and I wondered for about the millionth time who the woman had been and what had become of the baby she'd held. I was certain that the baby had been my sister who I hadn't remembered until the door had been opened and the memories had begun to return.

Chapter 2

Once I arrived at the peninsula, I grabbed the groceries I'd picked up while in town and headed toward my cottage. Kai and Kallie would be ready to go out by now. I figured I'd unpack the items I'd bought in town and then take a short walk along the beach. I'd arranged to meet Jemma, Josie, and Parker at six and didn't want to be late.

"Did you miss me?" I asked my two Bernese Mountain Dogs who must have heard me coming since they met me at the front door.

Both dogs wagged their tails and pranced around in greeting.

"I just need to put this stuff away, and then we'll take a walk," I assured them, as I set my grocery bags on the counter.

It was a beautiful fall day. Cool, with a hint of winter in the air, but bright and sunny as well. I wondered how much snow we'd get over the winter months. I'd asked a few people who'd replied that it varied widely from year to year. I knew that living by the sea didn't guarantee a white Christmas, but having lived most of my life in the south, I found myself longing for enough of the white stuff to add authenticity to the picture-perfect scenery.

I decided to head toward the right after I walked out onto the sand from the deck of my cottage. Cooper Fairchild rented the cottage to the right, and he was rarely home. He owned his own helicopter, which he used to provide tours and air charters. I'd been told that he worked a lot less during the winter months than he did the rest of the year, so I imagined I'd start seeing him around more often.

When I reached the edge of the peninsula, I looked across the bay toward Piney Point. The only corner of the house I could see from the beach where I stood was the southwest corner, which also happened to be the older section of the mansion and the section I seemed to remember from my childhood. In a way, it was amazing that I could remember anything at all. I still didn't know with a hundred percent certainty that I'd lived in the house on the point, but even if I had, I would have had to have been a toddler at the time since I'd been with my dad from the time I was around three. It didn't seem likely that a child who had been three at the time could remember much of anything about events that occurred twenty-five years ago.

Not that I remembered any events. Not really. What I remembered had been revealed to me as flashes. A stone entry that echoed with voices from the rooms beyond. Narrow windows that had been arched to frame the sea. A sunny porch with the trickling fountain where I'd pretended pieces of sea glass were baby birds who'd come to play. The images came as dreams I hadn't known were even real until I'd visited the house and saw with my own eyes that the pictures in my mind really existed.

I'd just turned to head back toward the cottage when my phone dinged, letting me know I had an incoming call. I took my cell out of my pocket and answered. "Uncle Gil," I greeted Gil Monroe, my father's ex-partner and best friend. "Thank you for calling back so quickly." I'd left a message that morning letting him know that I had some questions about my father and my past and hoped he could help me out.

"I'm always here for my little sweet pea," he answered, using the familiar nickname he'd given me a quarter of a century ago. "You still in Savannah?"

Gil had moved his family to Denver a decade ago, so the last time I'd seen him had been at my father's funeral.

"No. I'm in Washington State. A beautiful place called Gooseberry Bay."

"Washington? What are you doing all the way over there?"

"Actually, I'm looking for answers."

"Answers?"

I paused and gathered my thoughts. "A few months ago, I decided it was time to sell Dad's house. Of course, I had to get rid of all the stuff he'd been collecting over the course of the previous five decades before I could do that, and while I was working on the boxes in the attic, I found an old diary as well as a photo that seemed familiar."

Gil waited while I took a breath.

"The photo," I continued, "was of a woman and two small children. Both female. I'd say one was around three years in age, and the other was probably one." I swallowed as I tried to control the emotion that had begun to build just by talking about my find. "I'm not sure why I even took a second look at the photo. There was nothing spectacular about it, but for some reason, it drew me in, and shortly after I found the photo, I began having dreams about a house I was sure I'd never visited."

"But now you think the house is from your past. From before you went to live with your dad?" he asked.

"I do. It took me a while, but I was eventually able to track the house down. It's located on a bluff known as Piney Point, which is partially situated on Gooseberry Bay."

Gil didn't say a word. He didn't seem shocked or startled, which made me believe he already knew quite a bit about whatever it was that was really going on.

"After visiting the house on Piney Point, I now know for certain that I spent time there as a child. I suspect I'm the three-year-old in the photo, and I'm pretty sure the baby is my sister, Avery. I don't feel a connection to the woman in the photo the way I do to Avery, but I assume she might be our mother." A tear slipped down my cheek. "Or possibly an aunt or even a babysitter. I'm just not sure yet. What I do know is that my father found me alone in a burning warehouse on Christmas Eve when I was around three. I know he took me home and raised me. He was a wonderful man, who I love with all my heart, but after finding what I have, I'm beginning to suspect that perhaps the truth he told me wasn't the whole truth."

"You want to know if I know anything."

"Do you?" I asked, hoping he wouldn't totally shut me down. "You were his partner and best friend at the time this whole thing went down. It seems if he was going to confide in anyone, he would have confided in you."

Gil took a deep breath. I suspected he was taking a minute to decide what to say and what to keep to himself. If my dad had shared what had really happened with Gil, he would have sworn him to secrecy. Even though my father was dead, Gil was the sort of guy to keep a pact with his best friend. Eventually, he began to speak. "Marta had just had Susan that Christmas, so I was out on leave." Gil referred to his wife and oldest daughter. "Your dad was partnered with a man named Steve Burger while I was out. He didn't stick around long, so I never really got to know him, but I do seem to remember that your dad and Steve didn't really hit it off." He paused and then continued. "I came back to work around January fifteenth, and by that time, you were already living with your father. He told me the same story he told you. He said that he'd found you in a burning building and that he felt sorry for you, so he'd decided to keep you and raise you himself. As far as I can recall, he never specifically mentioned adoption, and I guess I didn't ask. You clung to him like a lifeline, and he didn't seem to mind. Your dad had never been the sort to settle down and make a commitment. He swore he'd never marry or have children, but then you came along, and suddenly he was about as committed as I'd ever seen anyone."

"But you don't know for certain that he ever formally adopted me?" I asked.

"No, I don't know for certain. If you're thinking that you somehow got lost in the shuffle after being found alone on Christmas Eve and that your dad decided to skip the formalities and give you a home, I think you could be right. Now keep in mind that I don't know for a fact if he legally adopted you or not. I never asked, and he never said as much. But it did occur to me that it was odd that there never seemed to be any sort of a process. I don't remember social workers coming around, and I don't remember any sort of court hearing. Your dad was a good man and a good cop. I'm not saying that he intentionally set out to break the law. What I am saying is that he felt something for you that Christmas Eve, so instead of dropping you at social services, he took you home. I'm saying that it's possible that once the holidays passed and everyone went back to work, somehow the fact that Patrick had you staying with him was overlooked and forgotten. Your dad never was one for paperwork and process. He was the sort who believed that what was right was right and what was wrong was wrong and the technicalities be damned. It wouldn't have been out of character for him to have simply done what he thought was best for you whether the courts agreed or not."

"So once he realized no one was missing me, he simply kept me rather than stirring up the beehive and taking the risk of losing me."

"That would be my guess." He took a breath and blew it out. "I want you to know that if for one minute I thought you'd be better off without Patrick, I would have said something. But the two of you were bonded in a way that was truly special. It would have killed you both if the courts decided a single cop wasn't the best match for a traumatized three-year-old."

"I'm glad you didn't say anything. I love my dad. He was the best dad anyone could ever want. If he had to cut corners in order to keep us together, I'm happy about that. But I do have to wonder how he happened to have the photo."

"Yeah," Gil sighed. "I've been noodling on that the whole time we've been talking. If he truly did find you in the middle of a burning building on Christmas Eve, and he really had no idea who you were or how you came to be there, then how did he happen to have a photo of you taken months before? That part makes no sense at all."

"Do you remember him looking for my identity?" I asked. "He told me later when I'd asked that he'd looked and looked but never could figure out who I was or where I'd come from. Do you remember him doing that? Searching?"

"No," Gil admitted. "Not really. I remember he told me that he couldn't figure out who you were, so he named you after his mother."

My name is Arial. The voice of the child I'd met this morning echoed through my mind.

Suddenly it hit me. I was *three years old* when my dad found me. When I'd asked three-year-old Arial her name, she'd replied without even having to think about it. It was true that I'd spent very little time around three-year-olds, which probably is why I'd never questioned my father's story before this, but apparently, three-year-olds knew their name.

"I was three years old when Dad found me," I voiced the thought I'd just had.

"Yeah. So?"

"You have children. How old were they when they first learned their name?"

Gil didn't answer. I wished I could see his face since I was certain he was frowning.

"By the time I was three, I would have known my name," I finally said when he still hadn't answered after quite a few seconds. "I'm not sure why I never realized that before."

"Yeah," Gil agreed, almost reluctantly. "You would have known your name, but maybe you were traumatized and wouldn't talk, or maybe the trauma caused you to forget."

"My dad never once mentioned that I had amnesia and couldn't remember who I was. He simply said he didn't know who I was and named me after his mother. I know my dad's last name was Holloway, so that part fits. Was his mother even named Ainsley?"

He blew out a breath. "I don't know. I never met anyone from Patrick's family. I think he mentioned that they'd been dead for a long time when we first met."

"He told me that his mother had recently died when he found me, which is why he named me after her." I paused to think about it. "When I was at the house, I remembered that my sister was named Avery. I haven't been able to confirm this, but I know it to be true. My memory is really fragmented, but I don't remember ever being called anything other than Ainsley." I closed my eyes and tried to remember back to the time I spent at the house on the bluff. I remembered the woman who I think I called Mama. Although, there were times when I tried to remember Mommy, and the woman who flashed into my mind was a different woman than the one in the photo. I remembered a man, but I didn't remember much about him. The only people I could clearly connect with were the baby, Avery, and Mr. Johnson, the groundskeeper, who had shown me where to hide my baby birds.

"So, do you think that Ainsley is your real name?" Gil asked.

"I think it might be. I have to admit I don't feel a sense of certainty about that, however. And if Ainsley is my real name, why would Dad tell me I was named after his mother? It would be easy enough for me to check, although I have to admit I never have."

"Yeah, it doesn't track that your dad would make that part up. Maybe you did know your name, but your dad had a reason for not wanting anyone to know that you were with him, so he changed it. You were three, so you most likely would have accepted the new name rather easily."

Okay, this entire conversation was freaking me out. If my dad had changed my name to protect me, then he must have known who I really was all along. "I'm beginning to think the story about the fire was made up."

"I will admit that something odd seems to have occurred, and there does seem to be a few holes in the story your father told both of us, but I know there was a fire," Gil countered. "On that exact Christmas Eve. Your dad and I had been working a case for months and getting nowhere. I know for a fact that your dad did follow up on a tip to check out the warehouse, and he did pick up a lead that led to the arrest of the man we'd been after. I don't know without a reasonable doubt that he found you at that warehouse. The best I can tell, if he did find you in the building, he simply took you home, and that was that."

"He told me he had a friend in social services who he called at the time. She told him I would go to a shelter over the holidays, and since he was willing to look after me, she allowed him to take me home that night."

"I suppose he might have been talking about Sherry."

"Sherry?" I asked.

"Sherry Young. She was a nice woman. A friend of both your dad and me. She worked for social services and was the sort of person who really cared about people. I think if your dad had called her and she had no way to process you that night, she would have allowed him to take you home until after the holidays."

"Maybe I should talk to her."

"You can't. Sherry died in a car accident two days after Christmas that same year."

I frowned. "Car accident? Single car?"

"Yes, she swerved off the road and hit a lamppost. She died due to blunt force trauma to the head."

Okay, now I was really freaking out. My dad told me a story about finding me in a fire. He'd told me he'd called a friend in social services who'd allowed him to take me home on Christmas Eve rather than taking me to a shelter. She died three days later, so she would have already been dead by the time everyone went back to work after New Year's. If my dad and Sherry were the only ones who knew he'd taken me in and she died, it would have been easy for him to keep me. But why had a single cop with a commitment phobia made the decision to take on the responsibility for a three-year-old girl? And even more importantly in my mind, had Sherry's accident been an accident, or had someone caused her to crash and had her death been murder?

Chapter 3

By the time the dogs and I made it back to the cottage, it was time to meet with Jemma, Josie, and Parker. The minute I opened the front door to Jemma and Josie's cottage, Damon and Stefan attacked me. It seemed my neighbors were huge fans of *The Vampire Diaries*, so when they named the new kittens in their lives, they'd decided on Damon for the black kitten and Stefan for the orange one.

I scooped up Damon while Stefan attacked Kai and Kallie. Luckily, neither dog seemed to mind a bit.

"Oh, good, you're here," Josie greeted. "Jemma's upstairs finishing up some work, and Parker just called, and she's on her way."

"Something smells wonderful."

"Lasagna."

"I thought we were doing takeout. Parker mentioned Chinese food."

"I decided that lasagna sounded better, and I had all the ingredients, so I called Parker and told her that I'd just cook. I hope that's okay. You do like lasagna, don't you?"

"I love lasagna," I answered. "I'm not sure I've ever had any that didn't come from a restaurant. It seems like it would be a lot of work."

"It is, but it's one of my favorites. If you like lasagna, you'll love mine. I use my grandmother's recipe, which in my opinion, is better than you can get at any restaurant."

"I can't wait to try it."

Josie automatically poured me a glass of wine, which I accepted.

"Is there anything I can do to help?" I asked.

"Actually, there is. I'm preparing a fruit and cheese tray since the lasagna won't be ready for a while. There are grapes soaking in the sink that can be dried and cut into small bunches. I washed the apples, but they need to be sliced. If you want to do that, I'll grab the cheese."

I grabbed the carving board from behind the canisters that were lined up by size on the counter and began slicing the apples. The only person I'd ever lived with other than my dad and my college roommate was my best friend, Keni, when we lived in New York. Neither she nor I cooked, so we mostly went out to eat. When I'd lived with Dad, it was mostly sandwiches and mac and cheese, and when I was in college, I mostly ate in the cafeteria.

"I'm anxious to hear what Parker has to say about the case she told us about last night," I said.

"Me too," Josie agreed as she began slicing cheese. "I remember the case from five years ago, but to be honest, I really didn't know the family and didn't pay a lot of attention to the whole thing. Of course, everyone was talking about it in the weeks after the family disappeared, but I didn't take a lot of time to think about it."

"I drove by the Hamish house today," I informed her. "I guess Parker's story really captured my imagination. What I found to be the oddest was the fact that the house is still empty. It seems odd that after so much time has passed that someone wouldn't have done something with the property."

"Yeah, I guess that is odd. I'm not sure why no one has ever sold the house," Josie said. "I guess it might be tied up in some sort of a probate situation." She paused. "I never heard if they found any next of kin. I guess they must have figured that all out by now." She gave both dogs a treat she'd had ready for them after they'd finished playing with the kittens and wandered into the kitchen to see what we were doing. "I guess we can ask Parker when she gets here. I'm sure she knows."

"Parker mentioned having notes," I agreed.

Josie nodded. "She told me that she has files and files of information. She really tried to figure this whole thing out five years ago, but she wasn't able to pull it all together. I didn't know Parker well back then, but I do know that she did a lot of digging at the time. She spoke to neighbors, co-workers, and friends of the children who were allowed to speak to her, although I also remember parents who were scared and kept their children reined in. She interviewed Deputy Todd. Parker really didn't know Jemma yet, so she didn't have access to her master hacking skills, and she didn't know you, so she didn't have access to your PI know-how. I think she's hoping that with the new team she has access to, she can figure out now what she couldn't figure out then."

"What do you think happened?" I asked.

Josie paused, holding the tip of the knife she was using in the air. "I'm not sure. I guess it feels like the family simply fled. I suppose they might have been kidnapped and forcefully removed from the property, but it seems that if that happened, there would have been some sort of evidence left behind."

I thought about bringing up my conversation with Vanessa Hudson about the blue sedan but decided to wait until everyone was here. "I had a similar thought," I replied instead. "I ran into Hope today while I was out at the Hamish place, and she mentioned that Gooseberry Bay is a good place to disappear if you really need to. After thinking about it, I realized that the place really is isolated. It must be a good thirty miles from the main highway that serves the peninsula, and it's a long drive or a ferry ride to reach any large cities. I have to wonder if perhaps the Hamish family wasn't hiding from someone who finally caught up to them."

"Perhaps. Hope is right about Gooseberry Bay being the sort of place where someone on the run might finally decide to settle," Josie agreed. "There's a cook at the bar and grill. Emily Brown. She showed up about a year ago with her daughter, Ashley, in tow. It was early in the day, before opening, so she knocked on the kitchen door that leads out to the alley. Tegan had shown up early to do breakfast prep, and I'd stopped by to have coffee and chat, so we let her in. Emily told Tegan that she was passing through town and had run out of money. She said she needed to find work for a few days and wondered if Tegan needed anyone to help out in the kitchen. She assured Tegan that she was a good cook, but also assured her that she'd be willing to do anything that needed to be done."

"It seems odd that she'd be passing through a town on a dead-end road leading to nowhere."

"Exactly," Josie said. "It seemed obvious to me that the passing through town thing was a ruse from the beginning. Everyone knows there is no passing through once you get this far south along Gooseberry Bay. Anyway, I remember watching Ashley as her mother spoke to Tegan. She was staring intently at some day-old pastries Tegan had left on the counter and planned to donate to the local church for their bible study. I could see that she was hungry, so I asked her mother if she could have one. Emily seemed relieved that I'd offered. I gave one to Ashley along with a glass of milk, and then I offered one to Emily along with a cup of coffee. Both mother and daughter ate those down as if they were starving. I think Tegan noticed as well because she asked Emily if she would be willing to make an omelet as a trial for a part-time cook position. She agreed. The omelet really was perfect, and after Tegan cut off a small bite and declared it as such, she cut what was left in half and offered it to Emily and Ashley, claiming she'd already eaten."

"I take it Tegan gave her a job," I said.

"She did. Emily asked to be paid in cash. She told Tegan that since she didn't have a bank account, she had no way to cash a check. Tegan is the sort who normally follows the dictates of the law when it comes to her employees, and she's meticulous about the payroll records she keeps, so I honestly thought she might turn her down. But she must have realized the woman was in real trouble since not only did she agree to pay Emily in cash, but she offered her three meals a day for both her and Ashley as part of her compensation package. She also gave her the use of the small apartment over the main dining room."

I raised a brow. "There's a second story?" I hadn't noticed when I'd been there.

"Yes. The man who used to own the building lived upstairs. Tegan was already settled here on the peninsula when she purchased the property, so she'd been using the space for storage. She cleaned it out, and Emily and Ashley have lived there ever since."

"What does Emily look like?" I asked. "I'm not sure I've ever seen her."

"She has short hair. Dark. Almost black. Her skin is fair, and her eyes are blue. Based on her skin tone, it seemed to me as if her hair had been died, although

Ashley has the same color hair, so in the beginning, I wasn't sure. Then Emily was sick for a week over the summer, so I went upstairs to check on her, and I noticed a thin line of blond at the roots. Emily does a good job of keeping both her roots as well as Ashley's touched up, but I guess she went a few days longer for a touch up than normal due to being ill. I didn't say anything, but she must have seen me notice her hair because she became flustered, and when she showed up for work the following day, her roots were dark."

"Does Ashley go to school?" I wondered. Talking someone into paying you under the table was one thing, but registering a child for school using a fake name was something else.

"No, but Emily makes sure she does her lessons. Tegan has a booth in the rear of the kitchen area where the staff can take a break. Whenever Emily is working, Ashley sits in the booth and either reads, works out math problems, or sometimes draws. She really is quite the artist even at her age. Everyone who works at the Rambling Rose loves Ashley, so we all stop and sit with her during our breaks. Harry, the bartender, tells her stories relating to local history. Sharlene, the hostess who works the breakfast shift, has been teaching her to do easy science experiments. Jemma has her working on the computer a couple days a week, and Tegan is teaching her to create new recipes that the two of them then try out. If the weather is nice, someone will volunteer to take her outside for a walk. All in all, I'd say she is getting an adequate education."

"How old is she?"

She shrugged. "I guess maybe seven."

"It must be hard for her not to have any friends her own age."

"I'm sure it is. Ashley doesn't have much freedom. I suspect whoever is after them is a real threat. Emily never leaves the kitchen when she's working. She eats at the restaurant. Tegan is good about buying extras like juice and milk for Emily to keep in the little refrigerator up in the apartment. I don't think she leaves the place very often, not even to grab supplies. I suppose she and Ashley might go out for walks from time to time, but they don't seem to socialize. I'm pretty sure the only people they have any sort of relationship with are the staff at the Rambling Rose."

"You don't think that Emily might be running from the law, do you?" I asked.

Josie shook her head. "I don't think so. Emily is sweet and quiet, and she works hard. I really doubt she's a fugitive. As I said before, I suspect she's running from a man. Probably a man who was violent toward her. She startles easily, and she's always looking over her shoulder."

"Wow," I said. "The poor thing. How awful it must be to know someone is out there who wants to do you or your child harm. I'm glad Tegan and everyone at the Rambling Rose are watching out for her."

"Oh, we are," Josie assured me. "If anyone ever comes snooping around, looking for either Emily or Ashley, the entire staff will be willing to jump in and hide them. Emily doesn't trust many people, but I think she'll like you. I'll introduce you the next time you're in during one of her shifts."

"Does she realize that you know she isn't who she says she is?"

Josie paused and then answered. "Well, it's not like I've ever said as much, but I suspect she knows that I've figured out that she may be running from someone. She's never admitted to me that she's not exactly who she presents herself to be, but Emily is a smart woman. I'm sure that she must realize by this point that she isn't exactly living a normal life and that those closest to her would have noticed."

"So it's one of those things no one talks about, but everyone knows."

"Well, not everyone, but everyone who works at the bar and grill realizes that Emily has a secret and we all respect that."

I thought about the woman in the photo I came to Gooseberry Bay to research. I thought about the fact that Gooseberry Bay was a good place to hide if you needed to get gone. Once again, I had to wonder if perhaps the woman I assumed was my mother had been on the run, trying desperately to hide from her own nightmare.

Jemma came downstairs just as Josie and I were finishing the cheese and fruit platter. She worked remotely for a company based in Seattle and kept an office upstairs, where she could be found a lot of the time.

"Is Parker on her way?" she asked, grabbing a slice of apple and a piece of cheddar cheese.

"She should be here any minute," Josie informed her.

She bent over to pick up Stefan. He swatted at her nose, and she smiled. "Did they ever find Damon and Stefan's mother?" she asked me.

"Actually, I got a call from the rescue just this morning. I guess they managed to catch two more kittens and the mother. They're going to continue to leave food in the traps for a few more days just to be sure they have all the kittens, but they seem pretty sure they have them all. They told me they even put the mama cat in a harness, which they attached to a lead, and then attached the lead to a tree. Once they were sure the mother couldn't simply take off, they hid behind some shrubs. They watched for almost two hours, but no other kittens showed up. It's their opinion that if there were additional kittens, they would have approached when the mama was left alone."

"Yeah. That seems likely," Jemma agreed. She held the kitten she was caressing up and looked him in the face. "Stefan here comes running anytime he even suspects there might be food involved in whatever anyone might be doing."

"He's lucky to have you," I said.

"We're the ones lucky to have him and Damon," she countered.

"It looks like Parker is heading up the path," Josie said. "I'll get her a glass of wine. Why don't you toss another log on the fire," she instructed Jemma.

I opened the door for Parker, who had her arms full of files. "What's all this?" I asked.

"Notes from five years ago. I have pages and pages of thoughts and impressions, transcripts of interviews, copies of maps and photographs, and computer searches that never panned out."

"You seem to have a good head start on the project," I said.

"At the time of the initial investigation, I thought I was getting somewhere, but in the end, none of my leads panned out." She accepted her wine glass from Josie. "I realize that it's going to be nearly impossible to pick up the trail after five years, especially given the fact that there wasn't much of a trail to follow back when it happened. But I have more experience now, and I have help I didn't have before, so I figured that nothing would be lost by taking a second look."

"I agree," Jemma said. "I'm ready to jump in."

"I'm in as well," I said. "As a private investigator, I know that not every case pans out, but this one is interesting, and, like you said, we really have nothing to lose by trying."

"So, where do we even start?" Josie asked.

Parker looked toward the stack of files she'd brought. "I thought we'd start with what we have. I can go through everything I found five years ago, and we can discuss which leads I tried to follow but ended up abandoning."

"That makes sense," Josie said. "Dinner will be ready in about forty-five minutes. I guess let's dig into the files now, and then we can continue to chat while we eat."

Parker started by going over the basic details, many of which she'd already mentioned the previous evening. "The whole thing started when Erma Gilroy, the neighbor living on the left of the Hamish home, came over on the day after Thanksgiving to bring the family a pie. I guess she'd made extras and decided to give a few to some of her neighbors. No one answered the door at the Hamish home when she knocked, so she left, assuming the family was out for the afternoon. When they still hadn't returned by that evening, she decided to peek inside through the windows."

"Didn't it occur to the neighbor that the family might have been out of town?" Jemma asked.

"No," Parker answered. "According to Mrs. Gilroy, who I was able to interview after the event, the family who lived next door mostly kept to themselves and rarely went anywhere. To work, school, or the store, sure, but she really didn't suspect they might have been out of town, especially after she noticed the food sitting out on the kitchen counter. She called the police. Initially, the police didn't want to respond since leaving food out on the counter wasn't a crime, but when no one showed up by the following day, Mrs. Gilroy convinced the police to break into the home, which was locked, and look around. Nothing was disturbed, but there was no sign of the family, either. As I said before, nothing was missing. The toothbrushes were still in the holders. The car was in the garage. Even Mrs. Hamish's purse was still in her bedroom."

"The food that had been prepared for the Thanksgiving meal was left on the counter," I said, basically, repeating what Parker had just said, but wanting to work it though in my mind. "From what you said yesterday, most of it was still in pots and heating pans, waiting to be placed in serving dishes."

"Yes," Parker answered. "That's correct."

"Is that important?" Josie asked.

"Maybe," I answered. "Was the oven still on?"

"No," Parker said. "Someone had turned it off."

"Was the turkey carved?" I asked.

Parker frowned. "I don't think so." She pulled the stack of files toward where she was sitting and pulled one out. She opened it to reveal a pile of photos. "I bribed the receptionist down at the police station to make these copies for me." She handed me a small stack of photos that showed the state of the kitchen when it was found.

I took a minute to study them.

"Is something wrong?" Josie asked. "You're frowning."

"These seem wrong."

"Wrong?" Parker asked.

I handed the photo on the top to Josie. "I'm no cook and have never made a Thanksgiving meal in my life, but doesn't this seem wrong to you?"

Josie looked at the photo. "Actually, yes," she said, narrowing her gaze. "The turkey is golden brown, yet uncarved. The potatoes are mashed, transferred to a serving bowl, and ready to serve, yet still on the counter. The green bean casserole has been cooked, as have the yams. Even the rolls are browned, although they're still on baking pans. If I was making this meal, I would have carved the turkey while the potatoes were boiling. I would have mashed them after the turkey was carved, and I wouldn't have placed the rolls in the oven to brown until the very end."

"Exactly," I agreed. "And where are the stuffing and the gravy?"

"I suppose that not everyone bothers with stuffing and gravy, and there might be families who carve the bird at the table and serve it as it's sliced," Jemma pointed out.

I supposed that was true.

"Even then, I would think that whoever made the meal would have transferred the turkey to a serving platter while the rolls browned," Josie said. "The way they have things here, the rolls would have been cold before the meal was served."

"I suppose the cook might have had a reason for preparing the individual items to be served in the order presented, but my first impression when I looked at the food on the counter was that it had been staged," I said. "It's like the meal had been cooked and posed intentionally. I mean, shouldn't there be dirty pots and pans? Look at the sink." I pointed to the sink in the photo. "Not a dirty pot, pan, dish, or utensil in sight. At the very least, there should have been a potato masher." I flipped through the photos. "The table is set perfectly and with a good degree of care. Linen napkins, matching glassware, and even fresh flowers." I nibbled on my bottom lip. "In addition to the flowers and six place settings, there are salt and pepper shakers, a plate for the butter, and a basket for the rolls. If the family planned to carve the turkey at the table, I'm not sure where they would have set it." I flipped back to the counter with the food. "It's a large turkey."

"Maybe the dad was going to stand at the counter and carve it as each piece was served," Parker suggested.

"Yeah. I guess," I agreed, even though I still felt something was off about the whole thing.

"So, what else do we know?" Josie asked.

I decided this was a good time to pop into the conversation with my news. "When I was at the Hamish house this morning, I spoke with a neighbor who told me that she'd been friends with Hannah, the oldest daughter. She told me that one of the neighbors had noticed a blue sedan parked on the street in front of the Hamish house a few times in the days before the family disappeared."

Parker raised a brow. "Really?"

"Do you remember there being any mention of the blue sedan when you investigated the first time?" I asked.

"Not that I remember." She took a minute to dig through the files. "Did this friend of Hannah's know if the neighbor she spoke to told the cops about the blue sedan?"

"She told me that she didn't know for certain."

"What was the name of Hannah's friend?" Parker asked.

"Vanessa Hudson."

Parker frowned. She opened a file and looked at her notes. It appeared like she was looking at a list of names. "I don't see a Vanessa Hudson on the list. Where did she say she lived?"

"She just said in the area. She said she'd been keeping an eye on the house." I paused to think about it. "She had a child with her. I assume she was her daughter, but I'm not sure. If Vanessa is married, her last name might not have been Hudson back when the event occurred."

"There isn't a Vanessa on my list, but I only have the names of people either I or the police talked to. I suppose that if she didn't live in one of the houses directly next to or across from the Hamish place, she might not have been interviewed."

"She said she knew Hannah. I guess they were in the same class in high school. I suppose we can look for a young blond-haired woman in the senior class named Vanessa. That should at least tell us if she had a different last name."

"I'll pull up the yearbook," Jemma said, getting up and crossing the room to her laptop.

While she did that, Parker slowly looked over her notes. "At the time of the incident, I spoke to all the closest neighbors. Mrs. Gilroy lived on the left, Mrs. Franktown on the right, and Carl and Connie Jeffries lived directly across the street. A vacant lot is to the right of the Jeffries, and then to the right of the lot is a house, which was owned and occupied by a man named Glen Burbank back then. He has since passed away, and the house has been sold. Barry Bonsworth owns the house to the left of the Jeffries. He still lives there. Old guy. Totally deaf. Said he didn't see or hear a thing. The Miller family owns the house to his left. Sam and Rosie have two children. Both boys. Both teens now, but they were in grade school back then." She opened and closed several files, taking a minute to scan the notes contained within. "I don't see mention of a blue sedan being seen in the area."

"Maybe whoever it was that Vanessa heard about the car from didn't think it was an important enough clue to mention," I said.

"Maybe," Parker said but didn't look convinced.

"I have the yearbook," Jemma said from the sofa where she was looking at her laptop. "I'll do a search for anyone named Vanessa."

The high school was a tiny school with only a hundred students, so it didn't take long to discover that there hadn't been anyone named Vanessa who'd been a junior or senior the year the Hamish family disappeared.

"How odd," I said. "Why would this woman walk up to me and introduce herself only to lie?"

"I don't know," Jemma said. "That really doesn't make sense. I guess you can go through it page by page and see if you recognize her, even though her name didn't come up. Did she mention anything else?"

"Other than the blue sedan, no, not really."

Jemma passed her laptop to me so I could look for the woman I'd spoken with. While I did that, the others continued to talk.

"So basically, what sort of conclusion did you come to five years ago?" Josie asked Parker after a brief break in the conversation. "Did you think the family left of their own free will, or did it seem as if the evidence pointed toward a forced abduction?"

"It was my opinion that the family was abducted. It seemed to me that if the family left of their own free will, even if they didn't have long to gather their things, they would have grabbed Mrs. Hamish's purse at the very least. It was as if they'd all been in the kitchen when whatever went down occurred, and they never made it back upstairs before vacating the home."

"I remember hearing that they had cadaver dogs go over the property behind the home, but they didn't find anything," Josie said. "Was there any evidence that the family left through the back gate, whether of their own free will or at gunpoint?"

"Evidence, no," Parker answered. "At least not as far as I know. I wasn't able to get ahold of the police report, so what I know is because I was able to bribe people to tell me what they'd overheard along the way."

"Was anything missing?" Jemma asked. "Phones? Computers? Winter jackets? Anything?"

"They never found Mr. Hamish's wallet," Parker answered. "Other than that, nothing was missing that I know of. You make a good point, however, about phones and jackets. I'm not sure if anyone looked for jackets, and it does seem like the two adults in the family should have had cell phones. I don't know if they were found."

"The reality is that the family could have taken clothing and personal possessions that wouldn't be missed, and no one would have even known they were missing," Josie pointed out.

"What about social media accounts?" I asked as I continued to look at the photos in the yearbook. "Hope said that the oldest of the four girls was seventeen. It stands to reason that she had some sort of social media account. Facebook? Twitter? Instagram? Snapchat? Something?"

Parker shook her head. "I couldn't find social media accounts for any of the members of the Hamish family. I was never able to identify any email accounts, although it seems like the parents and older children would have had them." She looked at Jemma. "Of course, I didn't have my secret weapon back then."

"It'll be close to impossible to find anything at this point," Jemma reminded her.

"But, you will look just to be sure there isn't anything to find, won't you?" Parker asked.

Jemma nodded. "I'll look."

"What about a landline?" I asked as I slowly scrolled through page after page. "Did the family have a landline we might be able to pull the records for?"

"Not that I know of," Parker said. "It is an avenue we can explore, however. Maybe one of the neighbors knows. Or Mark's boss. There must have been some way to get ahold of the family."

"Maybe when I'm done here, Jemma can pull up the school records," I said. "It seems that there should be both contact information and historical data. I understand the family only lived in Gooseberry Bay for a couple years before they disappeared."

"That's right," Parker said.

"Were you able to speak to Mark Hamish's employer?" Josie asked Parker.

"I tried, but he told me he'd been advised not to talk to the press."

Josie got up to check on the lasagna. Jemma got up to refill everyone's wine glass. I continued to look through the yearbook Jemma had pulled up on her laptop. I was about to give up when I had an idea. Instead of looking for Vanessa Hudson, I decided to look for Hannah Hamish. Her photo was missing from the headshots, which had been provided for pretty much every other student in the school. A search for her name prompted the reply that no matches had been found. I wondered if she'd simply been sick on picture day or if the fact that her photo was missing had been intentional.

"If the family left without taking anything, they must have left behind items that could provide clues. Photos and other keepsakes. Bills and financial records," Jemma said.

"Probably," Parker answered, "but I didn't have access to any of that. Most of what I know is because someone I interviewed shared a specific piece of information with me. I know that Hannah was a senior in high school and that Courtney was in the eighth grade. I know that Sarah was ten, and Laura was six. I picked up tidbits of little things about what each member of the family enjoyed doing as well as some personality traits for each. This helped me to formulate a picture in my mind, but didn't help me to determine what had happened to them."

"Dinner is ready," Josie announced. "Let's make our plates, and we can talk while we eat."

The others got up, but I continued to scroll through the yearbook. I really wasn't sure what I hoped to find since a search for both Hannah and

Vanessa hadn't turned up a single thing. I supposed my desire to try to find something in the book that helped to make sense of this whole thing could wait until after we ate.

I got up, served myself, and then took a seat at the dining table with the others. Once I was settled, I asked the question that had been filtering through my mind. "Does anyone know if the neighbors closest to the Hamish family noticed them at home earlier in the day on Thanksgiving Day?"

Parker shoveled a large bite of lasagna into her mouth before reaching for a file that she'd left on the table next to her plate. She opened the file and took out a sheet of paper. She swallowed and then took a drink of her water before she answered. "According to my notes, Mrs. Gilroy was asked about the last time she remembered seeing any member of the Hamish family, and she answered that the last time she remembered seeing any of them was on the Wednesday before the holiday. I guess there was a half-day of school, so Mrs. Hamish had taken off work early to pick the kids up from school. Mrs. Gilroy reported that she didn't remember seeing them after that, but assumed they were inside watching TV, doing homework, and getting ready for the holiday meal."

"And Mr. Hamish?" I asked.

Parker sorted through the file to a sheet of paper near the bottom of the stack. "Mrs. Gilroy didn't remember seeing him at all that day, but a man he worked with named Devon Butler told me that he'd dropped Mark off at home around five o'clock the evening before the holiday. The entire crew was off for a four-day weekend, and Mark had asked to take Monday off as well. He'd told his employer he had some business to take care of and could use the extra day. When Devon dropped Mark off at home, Devon reported that Mark waved to him and mentioned seeing him Tuesday. According to Devon, Mark was in a good mood and looking forward to the long break. Devon didn't think he seemed stressed."

"So, no one you spoke to claimed to have seen the family at all Thursday?" I asked.

Parker shook her head. "No one that I talked to. Mrs. Franktown reported that she hadn't noticed anyone in the family coming or going for several days, but both her kitchen and living room are at the back of the house, so she probably just hadn't been looking. As I've already indicated, Mrs. Gilroy saw the mom and kids come home Wednesday, but she swore that she never saw anyone from the family after that."

I returned my attention to the neighbors we all agreed lived in the area. Mrs. Gilroy had been the one to first notice the family was missing. On the one hand, it seemed odd that she hadn't seen a single member of the Hamish family after Mary and the girls came home Wednesday, but on the other hand, the houses weren't all that close together, and I guessed it was possible that everyone stayed inside once they got home from school and work. I asked if the drapes were opened or closed, but Parker didn't know. If the drapes at the front of the house were closed, then it would be very likely that the neighbor hadn't noticed anyone. I knew the windows at the back of the house had been uncovered. Otherwise, it would have been impossible for Mrs. Gilroy to have seen the food on the counter, which is what made her call the police in the first place.

"There was one sort of odd detail I made a note of that may or may not have been important," Parker said.

"Oh. And what was that?" I asked.

"Mrs. Hamish normally bought meal tickets for all four children every month."

"Meal tickets?" I asked.

"Our elementary and secondary schools share the same campus, although they are located in different buildings. The cafeteria is shared by the elementary, middle, and high school. A lot of kids bring sack lunches, but there is a hot lunch option that can be purchased with coupons that must be acquired in advance. Mrs. Hamish had bought meal tickets for her four daughters every month that school was in session since the very first month the family moved to town, but she didn't buy tickets for the December following the disappearance of the family."

"Maybe she was just going to buy them after the holiday break," I said.

Parker shook her head. "No, it doesn't work that way. The tickets for each month are sold at the end of the prior month and aren't available once the sales period is over. I suppose that's so the staff who work in the kitchen know in advance how many hot lunches they'll need. Anyway, the monthly tickets for December went on sale the Monday before the Thanksgiving holiday that year, and due to the holiday being late in the month, they were only going to be on sale until Wednesday of that same week. A woman named Betty Sutter runs the hot lunch program, and I guess she ran into Mrs. Hamish when she came to the campus to pick up the girls on the Wednesday before that fateful Thanksgiving. Betty wanted to be sure Mary knew that due to the holiday, the deadline to purchase the tickets had been moved up from the last Friday of the month to the last Wednesday of the month and wondered if she planned to buy meal tickets as was her custom. Mrs. Hamish thanked her for the reminder, but told her that she wouldn't need tickets for December."

"Maybe she just figured that December would be a short month, and the girls could brown bag it for a couple weeks," Josie said.

"Or maybe the early deadline threw her budget off," Jemma added.

"Maybe," Parker agreed. "But given what happened, I did find it interesting that she veered from her custom on the day before the family's disappearance."

Talking about the meal tickets reminded me that I wanted to finish looking through the yearbook before I left, so I pulled the laptop in front of me and continued to study each page.

"What exactly are you looking for?" Josie asked me.

"I don't know. I realize that neither Hannah nor Vanessa came up in a search, but I have a hunch."

"What sort of hunch?" she asked.

My brows shot up. "I think I found her."

"Found who?" Parker asked.

"Vanessa. Only her hair is different."

Josie, who was sitting next to me, leaned in, and Parker got up and crossed the room. I pointed to a young girl with dark hair who was standing with two other girls in front of a building that appeared to be the school library.

"That girl has dark hair. You said Vanessa's hair was blond," Josie pointed out.

"I guess she might have bleached it."

"That girl you are pointing out is Hannah Hamish," Parker said.

Now it was my turn to be shocked. "It is?"

She nodded and then headed back to where she'd left her files. She pulled out a photo of the family she must have obtained during her initial investigation. I looked at the oldest of the four girls and realized that with the exception of the change in hair color and the five added years, the woman I'd spoken to today looked an awful lot like the eldest Hamish daughter.

"Do you think Vanessa Hudson and Hannah Hamish are the same person?" I asked.

"If Vanessa looked like this, then yes," Parker answered, looking a lot more animated than she had at any point that evening.

"But how?" I asked. "And why? Even if Hannah is alive and living in the area under another name, why would she stop and talk to me? That part makes no sense. If her family was on the run, it makes no sense that she'd be anywhere within a thousand miles of the place."

"I don't know," Parker admitted. "Hannah was almost eighteen at the time the family disappeared. I have a note here from a friend of the family who told me that before moving to Gooseberry Bay, the family had moved around a lot. Maybe Hannah was tired of moving, so when the family fled, she decided to stay. Maybe she had a boyfriend and had plans to marry after graduation. Are there any senior boys with the last name of Hudson?"

I looked down at the laptop and did a search. "Yes. Kyle Hudson." I passed the laptop to Parker so she could take a look.

"It appears that I might want to track this Kyle Hudson down and have a chat with him."

"Do you think that Hannah's family fled from an unknown foe, and Hannah chose to stay for the boy?" I asked.

Parker shrugged. "I really don't know. At this point, I don't even know that the family fled. But if someone was after them, and if that someone was determined to do them harm, it would explain why they moved around so much. If Hannah was almost eighteen when the family fled, she might have decided that she was tired of running and opted to stay."

"Yeah," Josie said with a tone of doubt. "I'm not sure I buy the fact that not only did Hannah Hamish choose to stay behind when her family fled, but that she stopped to talk to Ainsley when she noticed her at the house today. Seems like a huge risk to take if she's supposed to be in hiding."

"I agree," I said.

"And where has she been all this time?" Josie asked. "There is no way she stayed in the same neighborhood. Folks would have noticed, even if she did bleach her hair."

"Yeah, I guess the idea that Vanessa is Hannah is a longshot," Parker admitted.

Suddenly I had a bad feeling. "I think we need to be careful. Just in case. I'd feel awful if Vanessa really is Hannah, and we put her in danger by digging around."

"Yeah," Parker agreed. "I don't want that either."

"Okay, I'm going to ask this again," Josie said. "If Vanessa is Hannah, why on earth would she stop and talk to Ainsley, and why would she just stand there in front of her old house and tell you about her family."

"Maybe she wanted Ainsley to know something," Jemma theorized.

"The blue sedan," I said. "Maybe she wanted someone to know about the blue sedan, but couldn't risk talking to anyone who might recognize her. I told her I was working with Parker. I told her we were relooking into the family's disappearance. Maybe she wants us to find the truth, so she gave us a clue."

"That seems like a pretty big risk to take," Josie said, still sounding doubtful.

"Maybe we're totally off track," I agreed. "But what if the blue sedan is an important clue? What if Hannah got away, but there were others in her family who didn't. What if she wants justice for those who died, or what if she hopes to find missing family members by tracking down the car she believes belonged to whoever took her family? I know that makes for a lot of *what-ifs*, but in the absence of facts, *what-ifs* are all we have."

Parker sat forward, resting her arms on her thighs as she appeared to be thinking things through. "Okay, let's assume, just for a minute, that Vanessa is Hannah, and she has a piece of information she's been dying to share. A piece of information that she feels might, in some way, help her family, whether it's to find justice for family members who were killed or to find clues that might lead to family members who were taken. She just happens to see Ainsley standing in front of the house and decides to approach her. Either she actually lives in the area, or she lives somewhere else and just happened to be driving by when Ainsley was standing there. My question is, why now? The family disappeared five years ago, and then, all of a sudden, from out of the blue, this woman decides to stop and talk to a stranger after all those years?"

"I guess it really doesn't make sense," I said. "Surely, if Vanessa really is Hannah, she would have found a way to pass on whatever information she might have long before this."

"Yeah, and the fact that she stopped and talked to you is odd, right?" Josie said.

"I guess." I looked at the photo of Hannah Hamish. "She did look a lot like the girl in this photo, but I guess it doesn't make sense that they're the same person. Maybe she just has similar features. And she did have a kid with her. Even if she did randomly drive by when I was there and finally decided to tell someone what she knew, it doesn't track that she'd spill the beans while standing outside the house she fled from with a three-year-old in tow. Besides, she walked down the street. I didn't see a car, although I did walk around to the rear of the house, so she could have driven by when I was in the backyard, saw my car parked at the curb, noticed the back gate was open, and decided to check it out. She might have parked around the block and then came strolling down the sidewalk as if she was just out for a walk. Still, the whole thing really doesn't make sense. Maybe Vanessa really was just a friend of Hannah's who happens to look a lot like her."

Parker stood up and began to pace around the room. "Okay, let's focus on the clue for a minute rather than the bearer of the clue. Vanessa told you she heard from a neighbor that a blue sedan had been parked in front of the Hamish home in the days before the family disappeared."

"Yes, that's what she told me."

"Okay, I need to ask the neighbors who still live in the area about the sedan. I'll do it tomorrow. Maybe we should meet again," Parker said.

"I told Tegan I'd provide a presence at the bar tomorrow night," Josie said. "Her weekend manager is off this week, and Tegan and Booker have plans, so she wanted to be off by six. She asked if I could cover from six to ten. I don't have to do anything other than be there in case there's a problem of some sort, so I can reserve that table back in the corner of the indoor/outdoor room for us. I can help you all theorize and be a presence at the same time."

"Fine with me," Parker said. "Is that okay with the two of you?" She looked at Jemma and me.

We both agreed that would be fine. After a bit of discussion, we agreed to have dinner at the bar. Josie thought it might be busy during the six o'clock hour, so we decided to meet at seven.

Chapter 4

The dream had returned, keeping me awake for much of the night. As they always had, this dream featured a young child playing on a sunny patio situated off a large room with arched windows that framed the sea. When I'd first come to Gooseberry Bay in search of answers to my past, I hadn't been certain that I'd actually visited the house in my dreams, but after a trip to the mansion on Piney Point, I now knew without a doubt that the house in my dreams had actually been based on a real structure. I still didn't know exactly when I'd spent time in the mansion on the bluff, but I suspected it would have been right around my third birthday.

The photo of a woman holding a baby standing next to a young girl had haunted me. While I didn't know it for a fact, my heart told me that the baby in the photo was my sister, Avery. She'd only been a toddler when the photo was taken. Actually, she looked to be no more than a year in age, so probably not a toddler at that point. Now that my mind had settled onto the idea that the baby and I were related, I couldn't get her out of my mind, and I couldn't help but wonder what had become of her. Was she still alive? I'd been found in a burning warehouse on the other side of the country just months after the photo had been taken. If I'd started here with my sister and the woman in the photo and somehow ended up alone in a burning building on Christmas Eve, I had to ask myself if a similar fate had befallen the baby.

My heart ached as I remembered my dreams. Unwilling to face the day quite yet, I pulled the covers over my head and closed my eyes. The dreams I'd experienced in the past had been different than the one I experienced last night. Before, I'd watched the scene unfold from afar in my dreams, but last night, I'd had the presence of mind to realize while still in the dream that the child I was watching was actually a memory of a younger me. I couldn't communicate with the child. At least not yet. All I could do was watch the same script that had played itself out over and over in my mind for months and wonder at the purpose of the whole thing.

It was odd, actually. While I experienced last night's dream from a vantage point outside the scene, watching the child rather than seeing the action of the child through her eyes, I could still feel the smooth surface of the baby birds as tiny hands cradled them, and I could still hear the sound of the sea and feel the warmth created by sunshine on her shoulders.

While the dream last night had been very much the same as those of the past few months, there had been differences as well. This time, there had been voices clearly understood. In the past, there had been voices, but they'd been communicated as sounds rather than words, or at least that's how I remembered them once I'd awakened.

"Ava."

I remembered a distant voice in my dream. It was a female voice that had sounded far away, as if someone had been calling out from the other side of a long dark tunnel, creating an echo that rumbled and rolled until it eventually faded away.

The child in my dream had looked up at the sound of that voice. Grabbing the small pieces of colorful sea glass she'd been playing with, she'd hidden behind the shrubbery. I could feel her tremble as she'd watched the woman who'd called out to her.

"Are you out here?" the tall blond-haired woman who had appeared in the doorway leading into the house had asked.

The child hadn't answered. She'd simply waited. It was an odd sort of dream since I'd been both an observer of the child and part of the narrative. I remember watching from afar, yet I'd also been able to experience the rise of the child's heart rate as she hid from the woman.

"Ava," the woman had called again. "We don't have time for this. If you're hiding, you need to come out."

The child had watched as another woman joined the first one in the doorway. While the first woman had long blond hair, the second woman had short dark hair, and she was carrying a crying baby in her arms. The child in my dreams knew the baby's name was Avery, although neither woman had said as much.

As I snuggled down under my heavy comforter, I remembered the dialogue that had played out in the mind of the child. She'd weighed the certainty of being punished for hiding against her need to take care of the baby birds tucked safely in her fisted hands.

Eventually, the women went back inside, and the child returned to the fountain where she'd washed each of her tiny birds in the trickling water. She smiled as each piece of glass sparkled in the sunlight, and I could remember her feeling of conviction that no matter what the consequence of her choice not to respond to the call right away, she'd always take care of her baby birds no matter what the cost.

I wondered about that as I slowly opened my eyes and stared at the blanket over my head. The feelings I remembered the child experiencing seemed to be mixed up with emotions that only an adult might feel. I supposed if the "I" in the experience consisted of both the memories created by the child and the experiences of the adult I'd become, then the experiences of the child in my dream might have been somewhat altered.

I closed my eyes and willed the memory of the dream to return. I latched onto the image of an old man with white hair and a weathered face as he arrived on the patio.

"There you are," he'd said, smiling at the child. "Everyone has been looking for you."

I remembered the child looking up at the man and then smiling at him. I remember feeling her pleasure at his arrival. Her fear for her baby birds dissipated as she held up wet hands filled with colorful objects. "I need to hide my baby birds," she'd said.

"I know just the place," the man had replied.

In last night's dream, I watched the same scene I'd witnessed dozens of times over the past few months. The old man had removed the stone at the base of the fountain and helped the child place the baby birds inside the secret compartment. He replaced the stone and assured the child that her baby birds would be safe, so she didn't need to worry about them. He then took the child's hand and led her into the house through the same door the tall blond-haired woman and the woman with the baby had been standing in just moments before.

I opened my eyes as it hit me for the first time. "Ava," I whispered. "My name is Ava."

I pulled the covers from over my face and looked at the ceiling of the cottage. It was still dark, but I could see that the sky outside the window had just begun to lighten. I closed my eyes again and wondered why I hadn't remembered that before. It was true the memories had come back to me in fragments, and I suspected that once I'd awakened, I'd only remembered a tiny part of the dreams I'd had. I'd known that the name of the baby in the dreams was Avery for days now, but the older child in the dreams had remained unnamed. Until now.

Ava.

I rolled the name around in my mind, trying to decide if it fit the way it should. The fit wasn't as comfortable as the name Ainsley, but it didn't feel grating, either. "Ava and Avery," I said aloud, causing both dogs to raise their heads and look at me. "It has a certain ring to it, don't you think?" Kallie barked once in reply before jumping down off the bed.

When Kai joined her on the floor, I realized that I couldn't lie about all day, so I crawled out from under the covers and made my way to the small bathroom. Once I'd washed up, I headed toward the kitchen to make a cup of coffee. Once it had brewed, I stepped out onto the deck, where I sipped my first cup of the day. Curling into the newly refinished Adirondack chair, I watched the sky turn from gray to pink. I continued to sip my coffee as the pink darkened to purple and eventually to red as the yellow globe of the new day's sun peeked from beyond the horizon. I loved so many things about my life in Gooseberry Bay, but two of the things I knew I'd remember the most were the quiet mornings and the colorful sunrises.

After I'd finished two cups of the hot brew, I got up and dressed in warm running clothes. I called the dogs, and we set out for our daily run through the forest and up onto the bluff. When I'd first awakened, I'd been so tired I'd been sure I'd need to go back to bed, but as I journeyed through the silent forest, I began to feel stronger, both mentally and physically.

As I ran along the narrow path, I allowed the name Ava to filter through my mind. I had to admit I wasn't certain what to do with that particular piece of information. The name felt familiar, yet I wouldn't go so far as to say that it felt natural. I supposed that even if Ava had been my name for the first three years of my life, the fact that Ainsley had been my name for the following twenty-five years would make it feel a bit more natural, despite how I'd started out.

As I climbed the hill to the bluff, I allowed myself to acknowledge both intrigue and terror. When I'd first found the photo of the woman with the two little girls, I was sure that the woman was my mother, but after last night's dream, I wasn't as certain. I hadn't actually been afraid of the woman with the long blond hair, I was certain of that, yet I had been afraid she might make me come inside before I was able to hide my baby birds. While she didn't feel like a mother, she didn't feel like an enemy, either. Maybe an aunt or a babysitter. Someone I knew and was okay with, yet not the woman who bore me.

Still, I remember calling someone Mommy. Someone else. Someone with a gentle presence and a soft voice. Someone I know in my heart, I would have shared my baby birds with rather than feeling the need to hide them. To protect them. To ensure that the bad man didn't get them.

Bad man.

The idea startled me, causing me to trip and stumble before I was able to regain my balance.

I didn't have an image to accompany the idea of a bad man but even thinking the words made my heart pound.

Had the bad man been after us? Was that why Avery and I had been at the house on the bluff with someone other than our mother? Was the bad man the reason I'd ended up in a burning warehouse three thousand miles away only a few months later?

I tried to remember, but it seemed the memories relating to that specific part of my past were still firmly locked behind whatever door I'd erected to protect myself.

As I jogged along the hard-packed dirt path, I thought about the other woman in my dream. The woman who came to the door holding the crying baby. She was new and hadn't appeared in my dreams before last night, and yet she felt familiar. I couldn't put a name with the face any more than I could put a name with the face of the blond-haired woman, but I somehow knew that over time a more complete picture would form.

By the time the dogs and I had returned to the cottage, I actually felt awake and refreshed. I decided to shower and head down to the boardwalk. The town of Gooseberry Bay was pretty quiet during the week this time of the year, but on every Saturday and Sunday, weather permitting, vendors with colorful carts sold local crafts and food products. The sun was high in the sky today, and while the air temperature was on the chilly side, locals and tourists alike bundled up and came out to buy a variety of products, including handcrafted holiday wreaths and other seasonal decors, freshly baked pies, and fresh produce.

Personally, I was excited to find that in addition to the traditional pumpkin and apple pies, the local vendor had blackberry and pecan as well. My dad had never been much of a cook, but he'd buy a pecan pie every Thanksgiving for us to share after a meal that usually consisted of frozen TV dinners featuring a main course of turkey. Each Thanksgiving, when he served the pie, he would tell me the story of his grandmother and the award-winning recipe she'd spent years developing, only to have it die with her after she'd neglected to write it down.

Deciding to buy the pie on my way back toward my car rather than carrying it, I bought a small cup of caramel apple ice cream to nibble on while I made my way along the wooden sidewalk. In my opinion, whoever came up with the idea of adding a boardwalk wide enough for mobile vendors on the bay side of the main street was a genius. It provided a festive atmosphere that felt a bit like an amusement park. In addition to crafts and food products, there were carts selling small toys and souvenirs that had the children as interested in browsing the temporary booths as the adults who flooded into town most weekends.

Of course, the cute and eclectic mom and pop shops that lined the street on the other side were a pretty big draw as well. In fact, I'd been told that the sidewalk was so packed during the summer and on weekends during the holiday season that you could barely make your way from shop to shop without having to step into the street. Which, I realized, was why the speed limit along this stretch of road was a whopping five miles an hour when the light was flashing as it was now.

"Booker," I said to Tegan's boyfriend and the occupant of cottage number two, as he walked across the street and joined me. "I figured you'd be working today."

"I am. I'm on my lunch break and decided to walk over to the boardwalk for a couple corn dogs." He looked toward the cart that sold corn dogs, fries, and regular hot dogs. "Are you hungry?"

I held up my almost empty ice cream cup. "Not really, but if you want some company while you eat, I'll grab a diet cola."

He smiled. "Great. I hate to eat alone. Normally, Jackson works the same weekends I do, and we just eat at the marina, but he's off today, and I felt like stretching my legs."

Once Booker had received the food he'd ordered, and I'd bought my cola, we headed toward the grassy area between the boardwalk and the water at this end of town and found a table.

"Tegan told me that you're working with Parker on the mysterious disappearance of the Hamish family," he said after taking a bite of his corndog, which he'd dipped in ketchup.

"I am. Josie and Jemma are too. Were you around back then?"

"No. I came to Gooseberry Bay about three years ago. There's a guy I work with, Noah. He would have been around back then. Noah has been around forever."

"I wonder if he'd be willing to chat with me. I know it's a longshot, but it occurred to me that the fastest way for the Hamish family to have fled, assuming they fled and weren't murdered or kidnapped, would have been by boat. Or helicopter, of course," I added, thinking of Coop's bird.

"Coop wasn't around back then. I can't think of any chopper charters that were, but I suppose you can ask Coop. He'd know. As for Noah, I'm sure he'd be happy to chat with you. In fact, if you want to walk back to the harbor with me, I'll introduce you."

"That'd be great." I smiled.

As it turned out, Noah was a chatty man in his late sixties who really had lived in the area forever. He seemed happy to have someone to listen to his tales, so once I got him started, it was difficult to rein him in and even more difficult to keep him on topic.

"So about boat rentals on the Thanksgiving Day the family disappeared," I brought him back on topic when he went off on a rant about kites of all things. "Would you still have records from back then?"

"We would, but we don't do boat rentals after November first. In fact, all the rental boats are dry-docked, so any needed maintenance or repairs can be done during the winter."

I looked out toward the harbor. "It sure seems like there are a lot of boats out there."

"A lot of folks who own boats, especially fishing boats, leave them in the water year-round. Then there are the weekend sailors who rent a buoy or slip for a night or two."

"So would the marina have been staffed on Thanksgiving Day?"

"Yeah. It would have been staffed. We actually get a lot of folks in town for the holidays. Most drive, but some come by water." He thought back. "I would have been working with Hook Wilder that weekend five years ago. Hook passed a couple years ago, but he worked this marina since he was a youngin, same as me." A look of sadness came over his face. "Hook and I would set up a grill near the office and BBQ us a turkey every year. Um, um. There's nothing quite like a turkey cooked over coals."

"Are you working alone this year?" I asked.

"No. A guy named Saul is working with me. Saul is an okay guy, but he doesn't really get the turkey tradition Hook and I had. When I mentioned cooking a turkey on the grill, he made a comment about just waiting to eat until after he got off. Guess he has a girlfriend in the area, and he plans to go to her place for dinner."

I wasn't sure what I was doing for Thanksgiving this year, although I did seem to remember Josie mentioning a get together at her place. I supposed I should confirm that with her. If the gang was planning a dinner, perhaps I'd suggest they invite Noah to participate as well.

"So, back to the Hamish family. It occurred to me that if the family fled of their own free will, they might have fled by boat. I'm not sure how we would ever be able to backtrack and figure out whose boat they might have left on, but I figured I'd ask if you happened to recall a boat leaving the harbor on Thanksgiving Day."

"Lot of boats coming in and out on a holiday weekend, but there is one boat that comes to mind. I doubt it was involved with whatever happened to that family, but I remember that Hook and I were sitting out on the dock waiting for the bird to cook when this huge schooner anchored about a quarter of a mile out from the marina entrance. The boat caught our eye not only because of its triple mast, but because it was an old gal that looked to have been restored.

"Did you see who was aboard?"

"No. No one ever came ashore. The boat showed up early Thursday, was anchored all day, and when I came into work Friday, it was gone. Not sure exactly when it left or where it was going."

"And you're sure the boat showed up five Thanksgivings ago?"

He paused and then nodded. "Yep. Hook was gone the past two Thanksgivings. This will be my third without him. And I remember the last Thanksgiving we spent together, which would have been four years ago, we kept a vigil waiting to see if the old ship would return. That means it had to have been here in the bay five years ago." Noah spat into the water. "If you're thinking that family fled on that ship, I sorta doubt it. I mean, it's possible, but they would need to have been shuttled out to it. It was a bigun. Wouldn't have been able to get much closer to shore than where she anchored."

"Thanks, Noah. I agree that it is unlikely that if the family fled by boat, they would flee in a huge ship such as that, but it might be worth looking into. I don't suppose you happen to know the name of the vessel?"

"Black Falcon. Dark boat with black sails with a red stripe."

I supposed that should be easy enough to look up.

I thanked Noah for the conversation and then headed back to my SUV. It seemed doubtful that I'd learned anything of importance from Noah. My conversation with him had left me feeling sort of sad. The poor guy had no one to have Thanksgiving dinner with, and it occurred to me that if not for the peninsula gang, I'd be alone this Thanksgiving as well.

Sliding into the driver's seat of my vehicle, I called my best friend, Keni. I doubted she'd pick up, but at that moment, I felt a strong need to speak to the one person who felt the most like family.

"Ainsley. How are you, girl?" Keni answered after only one ring.

"I'm fine. Missing you, but fine. How are things in New York?"

"Crazy busy, but that's nothing new. Did you figure out your origin story yet?"

I smiled. Leave it to Keni to refer to the story of my unknown past as my origin story. "Not yet. At least not entirely. I have made progress, however."

"Well, don't dawdle. Tell me all about it."

I spent the next twenty minutes filling her in on my visit to Piney Point on Monday, my conversation with Gil yesterday, and my realization that as a child of three, I must have known my name even though I'd lived my entire life never once questioning the fact that my dad had had no way of knowing who I'd been before he found me. I also shared the dream I'd had last night and the fact that I was pretty sure my name had actually been Ava.

"Wow, that *is* freaky," she agreed. "I'm not sure why I didn't realize the fact that at the very least, you would have known your name when your dad found you. My niece is three, and she not only knows her own name, but she knows the name of everyone she comes into daily contact with. She knows the name of the street she lives on and the name of her hometown. She knows the names of half the cartoon characters on TV and even some of her colors."

"The story my dad told me is one of those things I just felt like I'd always known. I've always known that my birth name wasn't Ainsley and that he changed it. He told me he named me after his mother, who had recently passed away. I assume that I didn't initially respond to the name, but as time went by, the name he gave me became my name, and I forgot about any other name I might have had, which I now suspect had been Ava."

"Why do you think he changed it?" Keni asked.

"I assume to protect me. Something bad happened to me. Something that ended with him finding me in a burning warehouse." I paused. "Or at least I guess that's what happened. I'm really not certain now. When I spoke to Gil, he did verify that there had been a fire and that the fire had led to the arrest of the man they'd been after, but I don't have any of the specifics." I took a breath. "I'm still not sure how my dad got ahold of the photo. Maybe I had it on me when he found me. Maybe the bad man the little girl from my dreams seems to be afraid of brought me to Georgia, or maybe the women I was with at the house on Piney Point brought me there, but the bad man found us once we arrived. I still have so many unanswered questions."

"Yeah," she agreed. "There are a lot of holes in the story. It does seem odd that you didn't remember having a sister before this."

"I suppose I must have missed my sister and maybe my mother at first, but if Dad didn't speak of them, I suppose I might have forgotten them."

"So, do you think the woman in the photo is your mother?"

I frowned. "I don't know. I feel a connection to the baby in the photo. I have from the beginning. But the woman doesn't feel like a mother. I know her.

She's shown up in my dreams, but she feels more like an aunt or a babysitter. Although..."

"Although?" Keni asked.

"I do remember referring to someone as Mama. Still, I don't think the woman in the picture is my mother." I shook my head as if the movement would rattle my thoughts into place. "I'm just not sure. It's all so fragmented. I'm not sure my dreams are even accurate."

"This is a lot to take in and process," Keni acknowledged. "My advice to you is to let it percolate. Your subconscious mind can work on it even if you're doing something else. Give your subconscious time to get everything filed in the correct folder."

I smiled. "I will. And thanks for listening. I needed to hear a familiar voice today."

"Any time. You know that I miss you."

"I know. I miss you too." I glanced out at the bay. "I don't suppose you'd want to fly out for a visit? You can stay with me, and I'll even pay for the plane ticket."

"You know I'd love to, but I have my play."

"How's that going?"

"Really well. But of course, you heard about Francisco and Natalia."

"No. I didn't hear. What's going on with Francisco and Natalia?"

Keni spent the next fifteen minutes filling me in on all the backstage gossip. By the time she hung up, I really did feel marginally better.

Chapter 5

By the time the group met that evening, I'd been able to refocus my thoughts away from the sordid past of Ainsley Holloway to the sordid past of the Hamish family. The more I learned about the family and the events leading up to and immediately subsequent to their disappearance, the more convinced I was that something very odd had occurred. When I arrived at the Rambling Rose, I found Jemma and Parker sitting in a booth in the back corner of the indoor/outdoor room. I'd noticed Josie chatting with one of the servers as I'd walked through, but I assumed she'd be joining us shortly.

"Beer?" Jemma asked, holding up an empty glass.

"Sure," I answered as she filled the glass from the pitcher. "It's busy tonight."

"There's a local crowd that gathers on the weekend, so it is always busy on Friday and Saturday nights even in the offseason," Jemma informed me.

I looked around the cozy room, which featured fixed walls on three sides and a wall of glass doors that rolled up to create an open wall on the fourth side. Tonight, the wall was down to keep the heat in, but on warmer days and evenings, it was usually rolled up.

"Tegan was lucky to find such a large building," I said.

"Actually, when she bought the place, the building only had one dining area," Parker said. "This room was just a covered patio, but Tegan had the idea of creating a four-season room by adding the walls to the sides and the glass doors to the back of the room. Of course, once she enclosed this room, she still wanted an actual outdoor patio for the summer crowd, so she built the deck off this room and then eventually added the picnic tables to the grassy area."

"Well, in my opinion, she has done an excellent job of creating the sort of space where locals and visitors alike will want to spend time."

I watched as Josie crossed the room and joined us.

"What did I miss?" she asked.

"Nothing," Jemma answered. "We were just talking about the remodel Tegan did when she bought the place."

"Did you dig up any new leads today?" Parker asked Jemma.

It did seem that Jemma had been assigned the bulk of the "tasks" we'd discussed the previous evening.

"I'm not sure if what I found can be categorized as a lead, but I did do a lot of digging, and am prepared to share what I know at this point."

"Okay, shoot," Parker said.

"First of all, the house the Hamish family lived in is owned by someone named John Smith," Jemma informed us. "I was unable to find an address or any other contact information relating to this particular John Smith, and the name is so common as to be useless."

"So, do you think the name might be an alias?" I asked.

"That would be my guess, but I honestly don't know that for certain. There doesn't seem to be a loan associated with the house. At least not one I could find."

"What happened to the personal possessions left behind by the Hamish family?" Josie asked.

"I'm not sure," Jemma admitted. "I guess that's something we might want to find out. I assume that someone cleaned the place out and that it's currently empty, but there aren't any windows that aren't either boarded up or shuttered to look through to verify that."

"I suppose the neighbors would know if someone had been by to move everything out," I said. "At this point, we don't even know if the family bought or rented, and if they did rent, if they rented the place already furnished or if they furnished it themselves."

"What about next of kin?" Josie asked.

"None were ever identified that I know of," Jemma answered. "At least I couldn't find mention of anyone. I did look for bank accounts and only found a single checking account. The balance was seventy-two dollars on the day the family disappeared, and the balance is twelve dollars now since there haven't been any deposits, but there has been a twelve dollar a year annual fee taken out each year."

I supposed a lot of families lived paycheck to paycheck and didn't have savings or investments, but it did seem a bit odd that there weren't financial records of any sort.

"I looked for cell records as well as landlines," Parker continued. "I couldn't find evidence of cell records for anyone in the family. If they had cell phones, they were unregistered burner phones. There was a landline associated with the house, and that was the number I found in the children's school files and in the employment files for both Mark and Mary. The phone was deactivated years ago."

"Sounds like a family in hiding," I said.

"It really does," Parker agreed.

"What about Vanessa Hudson?" I asked the question that had been tickling my mind all day.

"There isn't anyone named Vanessa Hudson listed in any local database I can find. I didn't have time to do a wider search, but I will. As for Kyle Hudson, he currently lives in Bellingham and is married to someone named Gwen. I found a number, but when I called it, the phone rang until voicemail picked up. I left a message. I guess we'll have to wait and see if he calls back."

"So the Kyle Hudson who went to school with Hannah Hamish is married to someone named Gwen," I confirmed.

"Yes," Jemma answered.

"Dang. I thought we might be onto something with the idea that Hannah actually had fled with her family only to return to Gooseberry Bay in order to be with her one true love."

"She might have, but if Hannah Hamish is Vanessa Hudson as we've theorized, it looks like it wasn't Kyle Hudson from Gooseberry High she came home to marry. As far as I can tell at this point, Vanessa Hudson doesn't exist. It might just be a name the woman pulled out of a mental hat when she decided to stop and speak to you."

"Yeah, probably," I sighed.

Josie looked at Jemma. "Did you ever find any social media accounts for any member of the Hamish family?"

She shook her head. "Not a one. And not only did the family have a zero social media footprint, other than the single checking account, they had no financial records, and they don't appear to have a history before showing up in Gooseberry Bay. I dug around quite a bit today, and I can't find a single mention of where they lived or worked or where the children went to school before they moved here. If I had to guess, Hamish was an alias. We discussed the fact that they might have been hiding from someone. After my research today, I really think that was the case."

"The question is," Parker said, "did they flee when they realized the person they were running from was closing in or did the person they were running from catch up with them before they could get away?"

None of us was willing to venture a guess at this point, but it did seem that if the bad guy had caught up with them, there would have been a struggle of some sort, and it seemed that someone who lived in the area would have seen or heard something if a skirmish had occurred.

"If the family left without taking anything, they must have left behind items that could provide clues. Photos and other keepsakes. I suppose the cops would have those items. I wonder how we can get a look at what they have," Josie said.

No one answered, and I imagined that was because no one knew.

The four of us refilled our glasses and placed an order for food before continuing the discussion. It was nice that I had people to dine with as often as I did. I didn't mind eating alone, but having someone to share a meal with was the superior option.

"Is there any way at all for us to track down the woman I spoke to?" I asked. "I still feel like getting to her might be the key to figuring this whole thing out."

"Maybe we can track the child even if we haven't been able to find the mother," Jemma suggested.

"I guess we can talk to the neighbors who live in the same area as the Hamish home and see if anyone knows of a blond-haired woman named Vanessa Hudson who may or may not have a daughter named Arial," Josie suggested.

"And I can check local preschools and daycare centers to see if I can find someone named Arial, but I'll need to be careful so as not to end up in jail for stalking a three-year-old," Jemma said.

"I've been thinking about it, and it seemed that the woman I spoke to really began to open up after I told her I was working with Parker. She told me that she's a fan of Parker's work." I looked at the woman I referred to. "Do you ever get fan mail? Maybe tips via mail or email from folks who want to pass along a suggestion or theory about a story you're covering?"

"Sure."

"What do you do with those pieces of correspondence?" I asked.

"Mostly ignore them. I'm a busy woman. I don't have time to read every email or piece of fan mail." She frowned. "Although in the beginning, before I became so cynical, I guess I did at least open all my mail." She looked at me. "Do you think someone could have written in with a tip? Someone such as this young woman who may have seen something, but was afraid to come forward."

"Maybe. Do you still have mail from back then?"

She shook her head. "A few things, but no, I didn't save most of it."

"Do you remember a tip about a blue sedan parked in front of the Hamish home?" I asked.

She slowly moved her head from left to right and then back again. "No. Not that I remember."

"It seems as if the woman who spoke to Ainsley might know more than she's shared. Maybe we need to widen our search," Jemma suggested. "I can do a search of the entire state, and if that doesn't turn anything up, I can add in bordering states. If this woman did just happen to be in the area with her three-year-old daughter, it seems that she most likely hadn't come from too far away."

Everyone agreed that finding the woman might be a good first step to figuring out why she stopped me and told me what she had in the first place. I thought about the photo I'd seen of Hannah. I thought about the woman I'd spoken to. If I had to guess, I really would say they were one and the same.

Chapter 6

Tuesday dawned dark and overcast. Several inches of rain had been predicted over the course of the next few days, although so far, all we'd had was a bit of drizzle. The dogs and I decided to head out for a walk before the heavy moisture blew in. I was tempted to take a run up to the bluff, but I hated the thought of being that far from home if the sky did decide to open up, so I decided a walk along the sandy shore of the peninsula would be a good alternative.

As I did most days when I chose to walk along the peninsula beach, I headed to the right. Three cottages were on the left, and I hated to disturb the others by walking past their doors so early in the morning, but Coop, the only resident with a cottage to the right, didn't seem to be home all that often even in the early morning hours.

As I walked along the sandy shore, I thought about the investigation the gang and I had undertaken. After my conversation with Vanessa Hudson, we'd decided to follow up on the lead relating to the blue sedan. Parker had gone through her notes in order to verify that no one had mentioned a blue sedan during the initial investigation, and then Parker and I had taken a walk around the neighborhood where the Hamish family had lived and chatted with as many neighbors as we could find at home. It seemed that no one we spoke to remembered anything about a blue sedan, which I supposed was odd. If a car had been parked in front of the Hamish family home in the days before their disappearance, it seemed that someone would remember having seen it.

I knew that Jemma and Parker continued to work on the case. Jemma had found her way into the official police files, but the digital copy of the investigator's report was sparse with only the very basic information provided. Jemma had also continued to search for Vanessa, but as of the last time I'd spoken to her, she hadn't had any luck. I could see that both Parker and Jemma were becoming frustrated with their lack of success, which made me feel bad for them, but while I wanted to help and planned to do so to the extent of my ability, the truth of the matter was I had my own mystery to try to find answers for. Answers I suspected I was going to need to find if I wanted freedom from the dreams that were disturbing my sleep nearly every night.

"Coop," I said as I rounded the corner and found the resident of cottage number five sitting on his waterfront deck. "I'm sorry to have disturbed you. I didn't think you'd be here."

"The mail charter I've been doing for the past few months is over, so I won't be going out as early in the mornings anymore." He looked off toward the dark sky. "With the weather that's being predicted over the next few days, I suppose I'll just hang out here at the cottage rather than trying to drum up some piece work."

"That's probably a good idea. I hear we're not only in for rain, but wind as well."

He held up a silver pot. "Coffee? It's fresh."

Normally, I would have continued on my way, wanting to get my mileage in while I could, but Coop was the neighbor I knew the least, and I'd never been given the opportunity to speak to him one on one.

"Sure," I said. "If you have an extra cup."

He stood up. "Have a seat. I'll grab one."

I sat down on a chair at the same patio table as he'd been sitting. The dogs settled onto the deck near where I was sitting. It was a cool morning, but I'd bundled up for my walk, so I was actually feeling rather toasty.

Coop returned with a large mug and filled it with the dark brew in the silver pot. "Cream?" he asked, holding up a carton.

"Thank you." I took the carton and poured a dollop into my mug. "So, you've been delivering mail in the mornings?"

"I picked up the mail here at the local post office as well as a few other small towns in the area and then flew it to the sorting center in Seattle where I picked up the mail destined for Gooseberry Bay and the surrounding communities. It's a route that's contracted by a buddy of mine, but he was in an auto accident and was out for a few months, so I temporarily took over for him. He's back now, so I'm done with the early morning runs."

"I guess it was good money."

"It was okay money, but to be honest, I prefer having my mornings to sort of ease into the day."

"I understand. I feel the same way. If possible, I like to run or at least walk in the mornings. I feel much more alert when I can get out and get some exercise first thing."

"I seem to remember you told me you moved here from Georgia."

I nodded. "I grew up in Savannah, moved to New York for a while, then back to Savannah, and then here. I've enjoyed every phase of my life, but so far, in terms of scenery and weather, this is my favorite overall environment."

"You picked a good time of year to show up."

I looked out over the choppy expanse of water that had been kicked up by the wind. "I understand you recently moved to the area too."

He nodded. "A little over a year ago."

"And where did you live before here?"

"Here and there."

I raised a brow but didn't push. I figured if he wanted to tell me, he would, and if he didn't, that was fine. The man didn't owe me anything. "So, have you owned your bird long?"

He shook his head. "I bought it from a friend just before I moved to the area."

"Really? I guess I figured you'd been flying for a while."

"I have." He took a sip of his coffee. "I learned to fly in the Army. When I got out, I found myself at loose ends, and really had no idea what I was going to do with myself. I have a friend from before I went in who does chopper tours in Hawaii. We got to chatting, and I told him I needed to find a way to settle into civilian life, and he told me he was looking to buy a larger bird and would sell me his old one for a really good price if I was interested. She only holds six people, including me, but she's got good bones, so I worked out a deal with my friend and then decided to move here."

"Why here?"

He shrugged. "I'd been to the area in the past and liked it. It's quiet and peaceful compared to most places I've lived or visited. The isolation was something I was looking for, and there wasn't a chopper tour in the area, so I visited the area to check it out, and while I was here, I met Hope. She introduced me to Bucky. Once I got a look at this cottage, I knew I was home."

I smiled at the handsome, dark-haired man. I'd felt the same way when I'd first set eyes on my cottage on the sea. I thought about the theme that seemed predominate as of late in which Gooseberry Bay was a good place to settle if you were running or hiding from someone or something. I didn't know Coop's story but based on what he hadn't said, I was willing to bet he had his own demons nipping at his heels.

"So, were you in the Army long?"

"Twelve years."

"Wow. That was quite a commitment."

He shrugged. "At the time, it didn't feel like a big deal. I spent most of those twelve years overseas, and to be honest, living on the edge and having important work to do really worked for me. I was in my element. I loved to fly, and I had brothers I cared about more than I cared about anyone I'd left behind. There was a point in my life when I couldn't imagine ever wanting to be a civilian, but things change."

"Yeah, I get that. Do you stay in touch with any of your friends from the Army?"

"Not really. I have a couple guys who shoot me an email every now and again, but to be honest, at this point, after everything that went down, most days, I'd just as soon forget that those twelve years even happened."

I was about to reply to that when he asked me about my life as a PI. I could see he was uncomfortable and wanted to change the subject, so I decided to let him.

"As I told everyone before, my dad was a cop. Even when I was a kid, he'd come home from work, and I'd ask him about his day. Most of the time, he'd tell me all about it as he made us a box of mac and cheese or a bologna sandwich. We'd sit at our little dining table, playing 'what's my theory.' I'd ask him questions about his case, which he'd answer, and then I'd offer a theory. He'd then poke holes in my theory and offer his own, which I then had a chance to rebut. We'd go back and forth a few times, each changing our own theories slightly to take into account any good points the other had made. It was fun and a good way to teach me about logic and thought process. After I got a bit older and was really able to understand the complexity of many of his cases, I'd sometimes come up with an angle he hadn't thought of that turned out to be helpful. Along the way, he began discussing almost all his really difficult cases with me."

"It sounds like it was a worthwhile activity for both of you."

"I think it was. Eventually, I moved to New York to pursue my dreams, but after he was shot and forced to retire, I moved home to help him with his detective agency. I was afraid he'd overdo it. Which he did. I guess I naively thought I could prevent from happening the very thing that eventually happened."

"I'm sure you did what you could."

"I did. And I cherish those years we had together. If he'd died when he was first shot, I would have missed out on so much."

I supposed I was starting to get choked up since Coop put his arm around me. We both sat in silence for a good twenty minutes before I got up and announced that I really needed to get back to the cottage and get ready for the busy day I had planned. Coop was the neighbor I had spent the least amount of time with, and thus he was the neighbor I'd known the least. I was glad that we'd had this time together.

When I arrived back at the cottage, I gave the dogs some food and water and then got ready to head into town for the volunteer meeting Hope had told me about. If I was going to live in Gooseberry Bay, even for a short span of time, I wanted to help out where I could and really be part of the community. It seemed that everywhere I looked, local merchants were already starting to decorate their storefronts for the upcoming Christmas holiday. In a way, it seemed early, but I supposed that putting up lights and trees and changing out window displays was a lot of work, so they wouldn't want to wait too long, or it would be hectic to get everything set up in time for the weekend festivities planned in December.

When I arrived at the community center where the meeting was to be held, the first thing I noticed was Hope chatting with the man I'd first met at the hardware store. I realized the fact that he was here and obviously knew Hope provided me the opportunity to confirm his name. The first time I'd met him, he'd been manning the paint counter at the hardware store while the owner was out. He'd pulled on a shirt to cover the jersey he'd been wearing, and the name on the shirt had been Mike. I guess in my mind that meant the man who'd helped me out that day must be Mike, but after I'd run into him while out hiking and he'd helped me to corral Damon, I realized the shirt he'd pulled on to protect the clothing he'd worn might not have been his. Of course, now that he'd both helped me with my paint and helped me rescue a kitten, it seemed awkward to ask his name. I figured I'd just wait until he finished talking to Hope and then ask her who she'd been talking to.

I waited from a distance and considered the fact that the man looked different today. Both times I'd previously run into him, he'd had something on his head that had partially covered his face. The first time we'd run into each other, he'd been wearing a baseball cap, and he'd had a riding helmet on the second time. But now that I was able to get a good look at him without a hat to shield his eyes, he sort of looked like…

"Ainsley," Hope waved at me, interrupting my musings. "I have someone I want you to meet."

There went my plan to confirm who the man was before speaking to him. I was committed now, so I started forward.

"Ainsley, this is Adam Winchester. Adam, this is Ainsley Holloway," Hope said, confirming my suspicion.

"I guess I never did introduce myself," he apologized.

"You've already met?" Hope looked confused.

"I helped Ainsley mix some paint when Hank was on a break," Adam answered, leaving out the part about the kitten.

"So you've chatted about her photo," Hope assumed.

"No," Adam answered. "Not yet. When I met Ainsley at the hardware store and then again in the forest, I hadn't talked to Archie. But once Archie filled me in, I had planned to arrange a meeting." He looked directly at me. "I guess we can take care of that now."

"Uh, sure." I knew I was probably staring, but I couldn't seem to help myself. "When would you like to meet?"

"How about after the volunteer meeting today? We can have lunch. Get to know one another a bit. You can tell me your story, and I can determine whether or not I know anything that might help you."

"Okay," I said, forcing a smile I didn't quite feel. I'd wanted to meet Adam Winchester ever since I'd arrived in Gooseberry Bay, but there was something in his eyes that I found to be disconcerting. Besides, the laid back and friendly guy who'd mixed my paint and helped me capture a kitten had been replaced by someone who seemed to be all business. Suddenly, I had the strangest need for fresh air. I looked at Hope. "I need to make a call. I'm going to step outside. I'll be back in a few minutes."

"Sure," she said, frowning. "Whatever you need to do."

I had to suppress my urge to run across the room and out the door.

Once I made it out into the fresh air, I took several deep breaths. I wasn't certain exactly where my near panic attack had come from, but I supposed it was the look of suspicion in Adam Winchester's eyes. I supposed I could understand that. The man was rich and probably highly sought after. I supposed the fact that some random girl had come into town with a story that involved his family and her possible involvement with that family might be a reason to make him cautious. Thinking back, however, I realized that he must have known who I was and what I was after from the beginning. I remembered the way his eyes hardened just a bit, and his expression shifted when I'd told him my name after he'd mixed my paint. Of course, he'd been back to his smiling, friendly self when I'd met him in the forest while he was riding his horse, and I was trying to catch a stray kitten.

There was no doubt about it. The man was hard to read. I knew my intent was pure, despite what he might think about the whole thing. I just hoped he'd listen to my story with an open mind once I had the chance to tell it.

Realizing that I was going to miss the meeting I'd come here to attend, I took a deep breath and headed back inside. Someone had set up rows of metal folding chairs for the surprisingly large number of people who'd turned out. I noticed Adam sitting between a tall woman with long black hair and a short woman with short blond hair. Both women were leaning in toward him and talking animatedly. It seemed as if both were intent on holding his attention. I sat down on a chair a few rows behind them, so I could watch the exchange without being seen. Adam was a good-looking guy. He was rich and single, and I imagined he was considered to be quite the catch. Given the fact there weren't a lot of single men in the area to choose from, I supposed Adam was used to being accosted by the single women in town when he came to these local town meetings.

Hope thanked everyone for coming and then went over the plans for Gooseberry Bay's Christmas Village, which was to be held December eighteenth through the twentieth. She filled the group in on the features from previous years the smaller planning committee had decided to continue as well as a couple new features that the committee was excited about trying out. I knew the purpose of this meeting was to get locals to commit to volunteer assignments. I wanted to do my part even though I was only a temporary resident, so I planned to offer to do whatever Hope most needed me to do. I knew that Tegan and Josie were already assigned the task of organizing the food for the three-day event. Neither of my neighbors was here today, but they'd had a separate meeting with Hope and had managed the food vendors for events in the past, so they were already dialed in. I thought Jemma might show, but I didn't see her in the crowd. I knew that Booker was helping with the boat parade, and I didn't know if Coop planned to volunteer or not.

Hope was about five minutes into her speech when Archie came in. He slid into an empty chair next to the woman I knew ran the local library. I seemed to remember Tegan saying that her name was Felicity Davis. She smiled when Archie sat down. It almost seemed as if she'd been saving a seat for him. Perhaps the two were friends. Archie seemed like a nice guy who had a lot of friends in town, and surprisingly, Adam seemed a lot more popular than I'd expected him to be.

Once the meeting was over and the volunteer sheet had been passed around, people began to disperse. Adam was chatting with Hope, and I wasn't certain what to do at this point, so I decided to help clean up the coffee and cookies someone had set out. I'd just carried the last of the empty trays to the kitchen when Adam walked up behind me.

"Are you ready?" he asked.

"I am," I confirmed. "My car is parked on the street out front. Should I just follow you to the restaurant?"

"Actually, we can walk. There's a pretty good café a few doors down. They specialize in local dairy and produce."

"Sounds good."

Adam placed his hand on the small of my back and motioned for me to proceed out the door. He then motioned toward a café a few doors down, and we set off side by side. Once we were seated, he jumped in by asking me about the photo he'd heard I'd been circulating. I pulled the photo from my wallet and showed it to him.

He took the photo and spent a minute studying it. His expression seemed to change several times before the man finally spoke. "Archie was right. This is the patio of the old wing."

"Yes. I was able to confirm that myself when I visited the property. Do you recognize the woman or children?" I asked.

He slowly shook his head. "No. None of the three seem familiar. Archie shared with me that he was pretty sure the photo was taken while we were in London for the summer. I find I have to agree with his assessment." He looked up from the photo. "Archie also shared that it's your opinion that you may be the older child in the photo."

I nodded.

"Do you mind sharing your story with me? I've heard parts of it from both Hope and Archie, but I'd like to hear what you have to say from your own perspective."

"Okay," I said. The man was somewhat intimidating, but his expression had softened a bit since we'd been talking, and there was a look of both interest and compassion in his eyes. "I guess my journey started when I was three years old." I went on to tell him about being found in a fire, growing up as the daughter of a cop, his injury and eventual death, and the photo that had brought me to Gooseberry Bay in the first place. When I got to the part about Mr. Johnson and the baby birds, Adam's smile widened, and his dark eyes sparkled in a manner that almost took my breath away.

"I take it you and Mr. Johnson were close," I said.

Adam nodded. "He was like a father to me." He paused. "Actually, I was closer to him than I was to my own father. Mr. Johnson lived and worked at the estate since before I was even born. He was the one constant in my life. My dad traveled a lot, and even when he was home, he wasn't overly interested in fishing, riding, archery, or any of the things Archie and I enjoyed doing. My mom was in Gooseberry Bay more often than my father was, but she spent a lot of time in Seattle. Mr. Johnson taught me to fish. He's the one who showed me how to throw and catch a ball, and I'm pretty sure he's the one who bought me my first baseball mitt. He was an important part of my life during my childhood, and I miss him every day."

"Archie mentioned that he's been gone for a while."

His expression softened. "Almost thirteen years. He passed away a couple years after my parents died. I know this is going to sound odd, but I think I took his loss harder than I did theirs. I'm not sure how much you remember about him, but he had this way about him. He seemed to know what I most needed to hear at the exact moment I needed to hear it. I trusted him. I leaned on him when things got rough. I sort of felt like he was my anchor."

"I get it," I said. "I had a similar relationship with my dad. And I do remember Mr. Johnson. The fragments of that time in my life have come to me slowly over time, but I remember feeling safe when Mr. Johnson was around. I remember trusting him even when I didn't trust the other adults in my life." I frowned. "I wish I could remember more. It's frustrating to have these tiny glimpses of a life I don't remember, but not to have the whole story."

"It does seem very odd indeed that you were here in Gooseberry Bay during the summer, and by the following Christmas, you were all the way across the country in Georgia. It's also odd you seemed to be with two women when you were here but were alone when you were found."

"And don't forget about Avery. The baby. Whatever could have happened to her?" I felt moisture behind my eyelids. "I keep thinking she must be dead, but in my heart, I hope she's alive." I took a deep breath and looked at Adam. "I understand that both you and Archie were in London when I would have been at the house on Piney Point with the women from my dream. I understand that while your father most likely is the person who allowed us to be there, he's gone now and cannot fill in any of the blanks. As is Mr. Johnson. But there must be someone who is still around today who would also have been around back then. Other employees? A close friend of the family? Even a delivery person who might have run into me while making his deliveries?"

Adam paused as if he was thinking over my question. I waited for him to share his thoughts. The server came by with our salads and refilled our water glasses before either of us spoke again.

"During the mid-nineteen-nineties, there were three staff members who lived on the property. Mr. Johnson, who lived in the cabin currently occupied by Moses, Mrs. Adaline, who used to cook for the family, and Mrs. Rivers, who managed the rest of the staff. The rest of the staff came from town and didn't live on the property. I can't really come up with names off the top of my head since maids and grounds crew tended to turn over pretty regularly, but I do have records and can find that information."

"I know Mr. Johnson has passed. What about Mrs. Adaline and Mrs. Rivers?"

"Mrs. Adaline married when I was around fifteen. She and her new husband moved to Texas, I think. I'm sure I have a forwarding address somewhere, although it has been a long time, so she may have moved again since then. After she left, my mother hired Ruth, who is still with Archie and me. Unfortunately, she wouldn't have been around when you were."

"And Mrs. Rivers?"

"She worked for the family until three years ago. She decided to retire and went to live with her sister. Archie and I decided not to replace her, so Ruth is the only one who currently lives in the house." He paused. "Mrs. Rivers might remember you. It would be worth a call to her. I have her number at home."

I smiled. "That would be great. Thank you. I can't tell you how much I appreciate your help."

"I can think of a few Gooseberry locals who would have been around back then and are still around now. I'll work on a list." He looked at his watch. "I have a meeting to get to this afternoon, but if you want to come by the house in a couple days, we can talk again. I should have a few answers for you by that point."

"Okay," I agreed. "Any time that's convenient with you is fine with me."

"How about Thursday? I understand you have two large dogs."

"Yes. Kai and Kallie. They're Bernese Mountain Dogs."

"Bring them along. We can introduce them to Hitchcock."

"Archie told me that you had a Tibetan Mastiff. I'd love to meet him."

"It's a date then. Come around noon. I'll have Ruth make us some lunch."

Adam didn't linger after we finished our salads. He paid the bill, walked me back to my SUV, and then waved goodbye as he set off on foot down the sidewalk. He certainly was an interesting man. One minute, he seemed brooding and intimidating, and the next, he'd light up like a Christmas tree, bringing life and color to the world in a way no one I had ever met in my life had been able to do quite as effectively. I was tempted to stop by the inn and get more background on the guy, but the dogs had been home alone for a long time already and would be waiting for me.

Chapter 7

Kai and Kallie met me at the door when I arrived back at the cottage. It had been drizzling off and on all day, but so far, all we'd really gotten were a few sprinkles. I'd brought an umbrella into town with me, but I'd ended up leaving it in the car. The first large drops of rain hadn't blown in until I'd reached the dirt road that took me from the main road leading out to the peninsula to the cottages that shared a single parking area.

I knew the dogs would need to go out, and I knew the rain would just get harder, so I pulled on a waterproof slicker and set out for the beach. Taking shelter under a large tree, I watched as the dogs chased each other up and down the sand. They, of course, didn't mind the rain a bit, but I didn't want them getting soaking wet, so once I felt they'd done what they needed to do, I called them, and we went inside where I tossed a couple logs into the fireplace and lit a match. Once that was accomplished, I made a cup of coffee. By the time it had brewed, the rain was already coming down much harder.

Settling in with a novel I'd bought ages ago but never had gotten around to reading, I curled up on the end of the sofa and tried to relax both my mind and body. After several minutes of trying to focus on the story, I finally got up and headed upstairs to the room at the top of the cottage that Uncle Bucky had used as an art studio. The room really was amazing. Small, to be sure, but the entire room was encircled with windows. Today, the sky was dark, and large drops of rain marred the windows, but on a clear day, it really did seem as if you could see forever. My plan at this point was to paint the room and set the space up as an office. I could totally picture myself sitting in this room, working on something I'd yet to define as life below the room made of windows continued to play itself out.

I'd just returned to the first floor of the cottage and was about to make another cup of coffee when my cell rang. "Hello." I hadn't recognized the number, and I usually let unrecognized numbers go straight to voicemail, but today I decided to pick up.

"Ainsley?"

"Vanessa?" I asked, unsure if the timid voice on the other end of the line was actually the woman I'd spoken to in front of the Hamish home the other day.

"Yes, it's me."

"I'm so glad you called." I smiled. "I've been hoping you would."

"I can't talk long. I really just wanted to know if you'd had a chance to look into the blue sedan I mentioned to you."

"I have, although I'm afraid I don't have any news to share. Parker looked through all her old notes and was unable to find anyone who'd mentioned a blue sedan during the initial investigation. Then the two of us canvassed the neighborhood on Sunday and spoke to those neighbors who were home. I'm afraid no one remembered seeing a blue sedan parked on the street during the week before the Hamish family disappeared."

"That's what I thought."

"You told me that a neighbor mentioned it to you. Would you be willing to tell me which neighbor that was?"

"It doesn't matter. I really need to go."

"Wait," I said, hoping I could figure out something to say to keep her from hanging up.

She didn't respond, but she didn't hang up either, so I continued.

"I really want to talk to you about what you might know. I understand that you might want to stay out of it, but I keep thinking you might know something important. Maybe even something you aren't aware that you know."

She still didn't answer.

"If you're willing to speak to me, I can keep your name out of it," I tried.

"I need to think about it. I'll call you back in a couple days."

With that, she hung up.

Well, I supposed that was something. If Vanessa and Hannah were the same person as I initially suggested they might be, it seemed like she might be ready to talk to someone about what she knew. If not, why would she have approached me in the first place? Parker wouldn't be happy about the whole anonymity thing. She'd already had to shelve a story she'd helped investigate relating to a murder a few weeks ago in order to protect the witness. The way things were looking, this story, even if we were able to resolve it, might be another one that she wouldn't be able to commit to ink and paper, which had been her objective in the first place.

After Vanessa hung up, I returned to the living room and sat down on the sofa. The rain and the wind had increased in intensity, making doing anything outdoors impossible. I had to admit that since I'd been here in Gooseberry Bay, I'd had very little downtime. I'd either been working on one mystery or another with the peninsula gang, or I'd been working on my own mystery, and when I hadn't been doing either, I'd been painting or settling in. And then, of course, there was the time I spent hiking and running with the dogs. I'd enjoyed it all, but I think this was the first time I found myself with absolutely nothing to do.

Which I supposed was nice, although I felt myself becoming antsy. Deciding to make use of my time, I gathered up my laundry and headed into town where I'd seen a laundromat. I'd noticed that Jemma and Josie had a laundry room in their cottage. There was plumbing in the little closet next to the bathroom with enough room for a stackable washer/dryer. Perhaps I'd look into buying something if I did decide to stay for the long haul.

By the time I'd washed, dried, and folded my laundry, it was time to head over to meet up with Jemma and Josie for our evening wine and cheese wind down. I'd even picked up wine and a deli platter while I was in town today. I'm not sure how Jemma, Josie, and I had settled into the nightly ritual, but it was one that the dogs and I looked forward to every day. Still, I didn't want to be presumptuous, so I had called Jemma to make sure that it was okay for the dogs and me to drop by that evening. As predicted, she said that she'd been planning on it.

"So, how was the meeting for the Christmas Village?" Jemma asked after I'd opened the wine I'd brought and poured us each a glass. Josie wasn't home from work yet, but Jemma had informed me that she was expecting her at any minute.

"It was good. I am pretty flexible, so I volunteered to fill in wherever Hope needs me. She's going to look at the hours and jobs everyone else volunteered for and let me know. She mentioned that Josie and Tegan are doing the food."

Jemma nodded. "They have taken over that part of the event for the past few years, and Hope knows I can be plugged in wherever. I think today's meeting was more for first-time volunteers to get an overview and those returning volunteers who still needed to sign up for a particular event or shift. Did you meet anyone new?"

"Actually, I met Adam Winchester."

Jemma's brow shot up. "Really? Adam was there? I'm somewhat surprised. He helps out every year, but Hope usually just calls him, and they discuss his contribution of time and resources over the phone. Either that or she goes out to his place so they can talk about it."

"Well, he was there today."

"Did you have the chance to talk to him?"

"Actually, I did." I told Jemma about our lunch and the brief conversation we'd shared. "Adam had a meeting he needed to get to, so he didn't linger after we ate, but he did invite me out to the house on Thursday so we could have a more in-depth conversation. In the meantime, he's going to talk to some people, and try to round up some information for me."

"That's wonderful." Jemma grinned. "Maybe he can help you figure out the final pieces that will allow you to really begin to understand what might have happened."

"I hope so. It would be nice to be able to make sense of the small pieces I currently have."

"Do you think you might try to find your sister?" she asked. "Assuming, of course, that you're able to pick up a trail of some sort."

I nodded. "Actually, if I can get a lead out of this whole thing, I do intend to follow it and see where it goes. At this point, I pretty much assume that my parents are dead since I didn't seem to have been with them while I was here in Gooseberry Bay, but I don't actually know that for certain."

"So, have you decided that the woman in the photo was definitely not your mother?"

"I don't think she was. The dreams are becoming more vivid, and the woman doesn't feel like a mother. I'm actually thinking she was a babysitter or an aunt."

"I suppose that would make sense. Do you still feel that the baby in the photo is your sister?"

Again, I nodded. "I do, and I'm sure her name was Avery. During the dream I had last night, I also think I figured out that my name was Ava."

"Ava?" She looked surprised. "Not Ainsley?"

"No. My dad told me that he'd named me Ainsley, which was his mother's name, and he gave me his last name, Holloway. It occurred to me that by the time I was three, I would have known my own name, so if my name was Ava and he'd asked me, I should have been able to tell him that. I suspect, given the fact that he changed my name, that I was in some sort of danger, and he figured that cutting all ties to Ava and her past was the best way to go."

"But you don't remember what sort of danger you might have been in?"

I shook my head. "No. I have no idea. I remember the flash of memory of myself with the baby birds on the patio. I remember going somewhere in the car with the baby and the woman with blond hair. I have these tiny pieces of the puzzle, but they don't, by any means, make up a whole."

"And what about after you were here in Gooseberry Bay on Piney Point? Do you remember any of it? Where you went next? How you ended up in Georgia? Who you were with?"

"No. I don't even remember being in a burning building, although that's what my dad told me occurred. My dad's old partner told me that there was a fire on that Christmas Eve. That doesn't prove that he found me in the burning building as he'd told me, but it could have happened that way." I paused and thought back to the conversation I'd had with Uncle Gil. "He also told me that if my dad had called a social worker, which is what he'd told me he'd done, it would most likely have been a friend of theirs named Sherry Young. Uncle Gil told me that she was a nice woman with good intentions who most likely would have allowed my dad to take me home on Christmas Eve if she wasn't able to place me in a home immediately."

"So maybe you should call her," Jemma suggested.

"That was my thought as well until I learned that she died in a vehicle accident two days after

Christmas the same year I was found in that burning building."

Jemma frowned. "Three days after she would have spoken to your father, assuming she was the person he called."

"Exactly. That makes me wonder if her accident was really an accident."

"Do you think someone killed her? Someone who was looking for you or maybe someone who didn't want you found?"

I shrugged. "Maybe. I have no proof. In fact, all I have is the conviction that the only person, other than my father, who even knew that he had me with him died before the new year when everyone went back to work."

"You don't think your father…"

"No. Of course not. Not Dad, but maybe her death was tied into whatever was going on. Maybe it really was just a horrible accident, but the timing seems suspect to me."

"Yeah, it is a little odd," Jemma agreed. "I know it occurred a long time ago, but maybe I can dig around and see if anything about her accident pops as being suspect."

"Thanks, I'd appreciate that. While you're digging, do you think you can discretely look around for any evidence that I was adopted? I don't want to open any sort of official inquiry until I know more, but I am curious."

"Absolutely."

"Also, see if you can find a record of me ever being in the system with social services as a child. I know it was a long time ago, and records weren't always digitized back then the way they are now, but it seems like there would be a file somewhere with either my name or maybe my dad's name attached to it."

"I'll look."

"And, Jemma, please be stealthy. I don't want to alert anyone to the fact that I'm digging around, and I don't want to do anything to sully my father's memory."

"I understand."

"Besides the fact that I wouldn't want to do anything to shed a negative light on my father, I don't want to do anything to stir up the wrong hornets' nest, either."

"What do you mean?"

"I suspect I was in some sort of danger back then, and I mostly feel that even if I was in danger then, I wouldn't be now. But the reality is we don't have the entire story, so there really isn't any way that I can know for certain whether or not the *bad man* from my childhood is still a threat to me as an adult."

"Do you think he might be?"

"I don't know. I hope not."

"I'll be careful not to leave a trail back to us," Jemma assured me. "I'll take my time and poke around slowly so that hopefully no one will even notice I was looking around in files I'm not exactly authorized to look around in."

"Thanks, Jemma. You're the best."

Josie showed up shortly after I'd finished filling Jemma in, which meant that I had to go over everything again. In a way, that wasn't a bad thing. The more times I went through it with the people in my life who I trusted to help me, the more solid the clues I'd picked up became in my mind. I will admit to feeling a little overwhelmed, but I also felt like I was a lot further along than I was a few weeks ago. Maybe by the time the new year dawned, I'd know who I'd been and how a child from Washington State had ended up all alone in a burning building in Georgia on Christmas Eve.

Once I'd exhausted the subject of my mysterious childhood, I changed the subject to the call I'd received from Vanessa.

"She called you?" Josie said. "Just like that? Out of the blue?"

I nodded. "I'm not totally surprised. A little surprised, maybe, but not totally. I seriously doubt that when she set out on Friday, she planned to talk to me or anyone else about the Hamish family, but I also suspect that once she realized I was working with Parker, she hoped I might be able to provide some information that she wants."

"Like what?" Josie asked.

"I'm not totally sure, but she seems really interested in the blue sedan. If she is Hannah as we suspect she might be, she took a risk by talking to me Friday. And then today, when she called me, her primary reason for having done so seemed to be to see if I'd found out anything about the blue sedan. She's definitely holding something back, but it really does seem that gaining additional information about that car is important to her."

"I don't suppose she told you anything else." Jemma queried.

"Not really. I did ask her if she might be willing to talk to me if I kept her name out of it. She told me that she'd think about it and call me back."

"Parker's going to love that," Jemma mumbled.

"Yeah," I sighed. "Even as I made the promise to keep her name out of things, it occurred to me that we've already asked Parker to do that this month, and maybe twice is asking too much. But even though Parker loves her job and wants to have the opportunity to be the first to print the news as it happens, she's also a good person who really wants the best for everyone. She chose not to tell what she knew to protect Sophia, and I think if she really believed that Vanessa was in danger, she'd do what she needed to do to protect her as well."

"I agree," Josie said. "Parker is the best. She'll grumble a bit once we bring up the fact that anything Vanessa tells you will be off the record, but I think she'll honor your promise as well."

Jemma got up and opened a second bottle of wine, and topped off everyone's glass.

"It would really be something to figure out what happened to that family after all this time," Josie said. "The disappearance of the Hamish family is one of the biggest unsolved mysteries in our area."

"It would be nice to have some answers," I agreed. "If Vanessa is Hannah, she probably knows the rest of the story, but even if she seemed to be a well-adjusted young woman and mother when I spoke to her, that doesn't mean that something really tragic didn't happen. If she is willing to tell her story, I think we should be prepared for anything."

"It is true that the way things are now is much easier to deal with than the *what-ifs*. I've settled on imagining that the family left of their own free will and that they're fine and living elsewhere. If Vanessa has proof that the family was murdered on that long ago Thanksgiving, it's going to be a hard pill to swallow," Jemma agreed.

"I guess if that is what happened, we'll deal with it at the time," I said. I took a sip of my wine. "When I spoke to Vanessa, I had the feeling she was protecting someone. If she is Hannah, and her family is dead, then there wouldn't be anyone left to protect. I guess if you think about it, it makes more sense that at least part of the family is alive and probably in hiding."

Again, I thought of Avery and me as young children. I thought of the women who seemed to have been with us. I thought about the reasons we might have been with those women. The longer I thought about what might have led to my eventual arrival in Georgia, the more certain I was that the real tragic story waiting to be told would end up being my own.

Chapter 8

Jemma, Josie, and I decided to meet with Parker today to go over everything we knew, including Vanessa and her call to me. Parker had plans that evening, so we decided to meet at the Rambling Rose for lunch. I wanted to be sure that we were all on the same page when it came to Vanessa's anonymity before she called me back, and I was forced to make a promise that wasn't only mine to keep.

"Try the soup and salad special," Tegan recommended as she took our orders. "The soup is pumpkin amaretto, which is to die for, and the salad is an autumn blend with pine nuts and cranberries. It comes with freshly baked bread."

"It really is good," Josie seconded.

"Okay, I'll have that," I said.

Everyone else agreed to the same suggestion.

"So tell me what you've managed to dig up," Parker said once our iced teas had been delivered.

I started by filling Parker in on my conversation with Vanessa. I explained that the only way I could get the young woman to even consider talking to me was to agree to keep her name out of things and that Parker would only use the pieces of information provided by her if she approved of them.

Parker frowned. I could see that she wasn't thrilled with the arrangement, but I could also see that she was resolved to the situation.

"But you did make it clear that I was still going to write a story of some sort, didn't you?" she asked.

"I did. I said that you wouldn't use any information provided by her in your story without her consent, but you are, of course, free to write about anything you've already managed to dig up."

"Which is nothing," she pointed out.

"True," I acknowledged. "But maybe once you hear what Vanessa has to say, you can work something out with her."

"So, do you really think this Vanessa is actually Hannah Hamish?" she asked.

I nodded. "I have reason to believe she might be, but to be honest, I don't know that for a fact. I do have a strong inclination to believe that she knows a lot more than she's shared so far. I just hope she calls back. She might not."

The conversation paused as the bread and salads were delivered. Parker buttered a piece of the still hot bread and then picked up the conversational thread. "I guess if the only way Vanessa will speak to you is if I promise anonymity on her part, then I will agree to those terms. I'll keep her name out of it, and I won't print any information that she provides that I hadn't already dug up on my own unless she agrees to let me print it."

"Great." I smiled. "I know this is a big ask, but the reality is that if you don't agree, she won't talk to me, and then we'll never know if she really does know anything."

"I agree, which is why I'm willing to make the deal." She took a bite of her salad. She looked at Jemma. "Any luck finding any of the information we discussed?"

Jemma filled her in on the details of her searches, which she'd already filled Josie and me in on last night. After she'd gone over all that information, she added the fact that in her opinion, not only was there every indication that the Hamish family had simply taken off, but based on what she'd found, or rather didn't find, it seemed as if they might have been running for a long time. Of course, this only made Parker even more interested in what Vanessa had to say. I really did hope she'd decide to trust us and call me back.

"So, how about your mystery?" Parker asked me when the subject of the Hamish family seemed to have been exhausted.

"I've actually found out a few things," I answered. I then spent the next fifteen minutes bringing Parker up to date. Like the others, she was fascinated with the possibilities. I just hoped she wouldn't decide to write about my mysterious past since I'd hate to ask her for a third time to keep everything we discussed off the record.

"I was able to find some information about Sherry Young's accident," Jemma jumped in when the conversation had worked its way around to the point where I shared the news I'd received from Uncle Gil.

"Oh, and what did you find?" I asked.

"As you'd been told, Sherry died in a single-car accident on December twenty-seventh, nineteen ninety-five. For reasons still unbeknownst to the investigator, she swerved from the road, hit a pole, and died at the scene. The accident occurred early in the morning. Around five a.m., according to the police report. No one came forward claiming to have witnessed the accident, so there's really no way to tell why Ms. Young swerved, but there wasn't any damage to the vehicle she was driving other than the damage to the front end caused by the accident, so it was never suspected that she might have been forcefully pushed off the road."

"That doesn't mean that another car might not have caused her to swerve," I pointed out.

"No. It doesn't mean that. There weren't any skid marks left on the pavement before the car veered from the road, so the theories at the time were that she fell asleep and didn't even know what was happening until it was too late, or she bent down to pick something up, or perhaps she was looking down to send a text and simply wandered from the pavement and lost control."

"So, no one suspected foul play." I verified.

"Not according to anything I found," Jemma said. "I didn't find any sort of report, police or otherwise, that mentioned your father finding you at the scene of the fire on the night he supposedly found you, either. There was a report filed by your father relating to the fire itself and to the subsequent arrest of the man your dad had been after in the first place, but nowhere in that report is finding a child mentioned."

Okay, that was odd. Really odd. If finding me in the building was not included in the report, and I actually had been in the building as my dad had told me, then he'd intentionally left that out. Why would he do that? Unless, of course, he had something to hide as I was beginning to suspect.

"What about my adoption papers?" I asked.

"I haven't found anything yet, but I'm still looking," Jemma said.

"And you haven't found anything relating to my situation as a child? Nothing with social services? No sort of report filed by Sherry Young?"

"Again, not yet," Jemma said. "Sherry Young was off work when the incident occurred. Everyone was. In fact, I didn't find a report of any sort filed by Ms. Young after December nineteenth. If she was going to file something about your dad finding you, I don't think she ever got around to it."

Which explained a lot, I realized. After Sherry died, my dad probably had seen an opportunity to simply keep me since no one even knew what had occurred or that he had me. It would also explain why he never mentioned finding me in the fire when he'd filed the report about the fire. Out of sight, out of mind. I still couldn't reconcile the *why* in my mind, but I think I was beginning to understand the question of how a single cop had been allowed to adopt the three-year-old girl he'd found one Christmas Eve night.

Chapter 9

As it turned out, Vanessa called me back a lot sooner than I'd expected she would. She'd said she'd need a couple days to think things over, but the reality was it had barely been twenty-four hours since her previous call. I was sitting at my dining table, answering emails as I watched it rain, so I logged off and answered.

"Vanessa?"

"Yes, it's me. Did you speak to Parker and the others?"

"I did." I got up and crossed the room to the sofa. "They all agreed to keep anything you might tell me in confidence. Parker still plans to do a story about the disappearance of the Hamish family, but she agreed to keep your name out of it. If you provide any information she couldn't have learned on her own, and you ask her to keep it out of the article, she will honor your request."

"Okay." She blew out a breath. "I guess I'll need to trust you."

"Before we begin, I want to remind you that no one is forcing you to speak to me if you're uncomfortable with this."

"I know. But I think you might be able to help me, and I realize that the only way I'm going to really be able to ask for the help I'm after is if I'm straight with you."

"Okay. I'm listening."

"I guess you've figured out by now that I'm Hannah."

"We suspected as much," I confirmed.

She paused, taking one last breath, which she seemed to hold for longer than might be considered normal. "It all started about five years before the Thanksgiving when the family living in Gooseberry Bay went missing, which would make it ten years before now," Vanessa began in a soft voice. She seemed to be struggling. I suspected she was working out exactly what she wanted to say as she said it. "My youngest sister had just turned one, and my parents had formally decided there wouldn't be any new additions to the family, so Mom and Dad sat down and discussed their hopes and dreams for the future. To this point, Mom had always stayed home with us, and my dad had always worked two jobs to make ends meet."

She paused again, and again, I quietly waited.

"My father had always wanted to go to law school, but with four children, there never seemed to be time or money to accommodate such a big dream," she continued. "My mom decided that once my baby sister was old enough for daycare, she'd get a job, and my dad could quit his second job as a janitor at the largest law firm in Houston, which is where we lived at the time."

I could hear something in the background. Paper rustling? I didn't want to interrupt Vanessa's flow now that she seemed to have gotten started, so I didn't ask about it. When she still didn't continue after a full minute, I decided to prompt her by asking what had happened after her mom and dad talked about him quitting his night job.

"It's sort of a long story."

"It's okay. Take your time, and work it out as you go."

"Okay," she said before pausing again and then continuing. "I was only thirteen at the time, and there might be gaps in my story since I didn't have access to all the details. Based on what I've been told over time, my dad had been working his regular night shift when he happened to hear the senior partner in the firm having a conversation with one of his clients. This particular client was not only very rich and well connected, but it was a well-known fact that the man had political aspirations. There was even talk of a run for president at some point in the very distant future."

I didn't ask who it was she was speaking about since I didn't want to interrupt her just as she was getting started with her story, but I had to admit I was curious.

"Anyway," she continued, "my dad decided to wait to clean the conference room until the men had finished their meeting but as he turned to walk away, he heard something that caused him to pause and listen. It seemed that this very prominent client had strayed from his marriage vows, and apparently, he'd managed to get his much younger mistress pregnant. Now, this particular client was well known in the area for his stance on family values, so my dad realized right away that if the conversation being held between the client and his attorney was made public, it would cause all sorts of problems for the man who wanted to one day to live in the White House."

"Wow, I can imagine," I said. "What happened after that?"

"My father quite unwisely continued to listen in. The door to the conference room had been left open, so it was easy to hear what was being said without being seen since Dad stood just beyond the open door. Additionally, it was late in the evening, so the entire floor was empty other than these two men and my father. Obviously, no one was worried about my dad overhearing the conversation since no one had bothered to close the door. I've wondered about that over the years, but I guess it's true what they say about janitors and waitresses. It's like people just look right through them, never even noticing their presence as they go about their business."

"Yes, I've noticed that as well. I waited tables for a while in high school, and there were several occasions when I'd come by to refill water glasses only to overhear details of extremely intimate conversations. Anyway, go on with your story."

She began to speak. "As I said, my dad paused to listen, and what he heard ended up changing the entire trajectory of our lives."

"Changing it, how?" I asked.

"Well, apparently, this very connected client was in a bit of trouble. It seemed that not only had the client found out that his pregnant mistress planned to cash in on the child she was carrying by asking for support, but I guess she'd also threatened to go public with the name of the baby's father if he didn't provide a bit extra to the compensation package."

"So she was blackmailing him."

"Basically."

"So what did the client want? Was he looking for financial advice?"

"No. Not financial advice. It gets a bit more complicated."

"Okay. Go on."

"Based on what my father overheard, it sounded like the client had confronted this woman about her apparent blackmail scheme, and in the course of discussing his options with her, he'd ended up killing her."

I gasped. "Killing?"

"I don't think it was planned. Like I said, I was only thirteen, so I wasn't privy to every detail, but I did overhear my mom and my dad talking at one point, and based on what I could put together, it sounded as if this very rich wannabee politician knew that he'd be ruined if word of his love child was leaked."

"Well, sure. Especially if his platform was based on family values. But to kill the woman? That seems like a bit of an overreaction."

"I don't think he meant to kill her. It sounded as if the client got mad and pushed the woman, and she hit her head.

I closed my eyes, stifling a groan. I was pretty sure I knew exactly where this story was going.

"The client admitted that he freaked out and went a little crazy. The woman had been knocked out after her fall, but at that point, she was very much alive. Apparently, the client was terrified of being found out and decided to ensure that the woman was unable to tell her story, so he strangled her while she was unconscious."

It was at this point that a tiny gasp escaped my closed lips.

"Ainsley?"

"I'm here," I said. "And I'm listening. Go on."

"Anyway, based on what I've managed to find out, the wannabe politician panicked and hid the body. At that point, no one knew the woman was dead or even missing. The senior partner in the law firm, who was apparently also the man's friend, agreed to help him clean up his mess so that no one would ever know what happened. When the men got up from the table where they'd been talking, my dad skedaddled, so he wasn't entirely certain what came next. But then a week later, the woman's body was found in a shallow grave, and a week after that, the woman's boyfriend was arrested for murder. The cops just assumed the baby was his and that the two had fought, and during the course of that fight, he'd killed her."

"Of course, your dad knew the truth," I said.

"He did. He felt bad for the boyfriend, so he decided to look around to see if he could find any sort of proof that might back up the truth, as he knew it. Without proof, he knew that if he came forward, it would simply be his word against the word of two very wealthy and well-connected men in the community. Being a janitor, he had access to all the offices, and he was often alone at night, although he didn't have access to computers and file cabinets. Still, he figured he'd look around and hope to catch a break."

"And did he find what he was looking for?" I asked.

"Yes, he eventually found a tape recording the senior partner had made when he'd met with his client on that first night in the conference room."

"He kept a tape?"

"My dad said he kept a tape of all his conversations. Insurance, I guess, or maybe he wanted to have a way to recheck what was said after the fact."

"Okay. I guess that makes sense. So, how did your dad get ahold of the tape?"

"Apparently, this senior partner was working late on the same night that my dad was on the floor cleaning. My dad avoided his office, deciding to wait until he left to clean, but he did check back from time to time to see if the coast was clear. One of those times when he checked back, he noticed that the door was open, but the office was empty. He figured the man had gone to the men's room or maybe to the breakroom for coffee or a cigarette. Anyway, my dad was about to move on with plans to return later to empty trash and clean up when he noticed that one of the file cabinets had been left open. It was at this point that he slipped in and quickly took a look for a file with the name of the client he'd overheard that first night."

"Seems gutsy."

"Or crazy," Vanessa countered. "Anyway, my dad found the file he was looking for, and inside the file was a small cassette tape. My dad unwisely took it and then quickly left. He finished his shift and then went home."

"What did he do with the tape?" I asked.

"Nothing at first. I don't think he was quite sure what to do with it. No one seemed to know it was missing. I suppose by this point, the senior partner's client had probably figured he'd gotten away with murder, so the heat was off. The boyfriend of the dead woman was in jail awaiting trial for murder. If I had to guess, no one knew my dad had taken the tape because no one had gone looking for it to even know that it was missing."

"But I'm sensing this changed."

"Yes." She cleared her throat. "My dad didn't want to bring attention to himself, but he didn't want the boyfriend to spend his life in prison for a murder he didn't commit, either, so he had the idea to send the tape to a journalist known in the area for publishing these type of exposés. My dad copied the tape and then sent the original to this journalist anonymously. The journalist took some time to dig into things, but eventually, the journalist printed the story, and the whole mess was brought to light. The problem was that somehow, someone must have figured out who'd leaked the news in the first place because a few weeks after the story ran, there was an attempt made on my father's life."

"What sort of attempt?"

"He was shot in the back while walking to his car in the parking garage near his day job. He obviously didn't die, but he could have. It was at that point that my parents decided to run."

The story made perfect sense, although I still had no idea how all of that led to the disappearance from

Gooseberry Bay five Thanksgivings ago. "Okay, I'm following," I said. "Go on."

"After my father was released from the hospital, my parents grabbed all the cash they could get their hands on, and then the six of us snuck away in the middle of the night. We moved around a lot for the next two years, rarely staying in any one place for more than a few weeks before moving on again. I'm not sure if the wannabe politician who'd killed his mistress, or anyone else involved in the case, was actually after us, but my dad had become paranoid after being shot and left for dead, and he was constantly looking over his shoulder. If someone even looked at him funny, he was packing us up, and we were once again taking to the road."

"That must have been hard on all of you."

"It was. We weren't allowed to go to school or have friends, and my dad kept changing our names. Half the time, I couldn't even remember what my current name was supposed to be. It was awful. But then we came to Gooseberry Bay, and my dad began to relax. After a while, he even let us go to school. I was happy for the first time in a long time. We all were. I really thought that maybe we'd be able to live a regular life, but then my dad noticed a blue sedan parked on our street, and his paranoia came back. Before I even knew what was happening, he was gathering up his cash and preparing to move us again."

"You must have been so upset."

"I was devastated. I had friends and a boyfriend. I was almost eighteen and knew that in a few months, I could begin making my own decisions. I loved my family, but I hated my life, and I figured that if I left my family, I'd be safe. The bad man, if there even was one, which, trust me, I was less than certain of by this point, was, after all, after my dad and not me. I decided that if I set out on my own, I could finally be free."

"So, what happened?" I asked. "Did you separate from your family?"

"Eventually, but not yet," she answered. "Let me back up a bit to the point where my dad first noticed the blue car. When he brought it up, I tried to tell him that a lot of people parked on the street when visiting friends in the area and that just because someone had parked in front of our house, that didn't mean they were looking for or watching us. My very paranoid father, however, was absolutely certain that the blue sedan had been in the area to find us, and that the only choice we had was to run again."

She paused. I could hear her breathing heavily. It sounded like she was crying.

"I tried to tell him that it was very unlikely that anyone was here for us, but there was no reasoning with him. He assured me that this very powerful man had tried to kill him once and would try again. I made the point that if the people in the blue sedan were here to kill him, they'd just get on with it and wouldn't be sitting around watching us, but he had this whole conspiracy story that he'd created in his imagination, and he was sure they were just waiting for the right time."

"I'm so sorry. That must have been awful."

"It was."

"Did your mom seem to think there were people in the area, just waiting to pounce?"

"I don't think she was as certain as my father, but she loved him, and he had almost died, and I think she'd decided to support him no matter what. If he said run, then she was darn well going to pack us up and run."

I supposed I could understand that to a point.

"Anyway," Vanessa continued, "since there is only one way in and out of the area, actually two if you include car and boat, but only one way by road, my dad felt it was necessary to come up with an elaborate plan. There are those traffic cameras as you merge onto the bridge, so he felt that once the man who was after him realized the family had fled, they'd access those cameras in order to look for the vehicle we escaped in. My mom came up with the idea of leaving behind evidence that made it appear as if we disappeared just as we were sitting down to our Thanksgiving meal so that this guy my dad was sure was after us would look at the tapes from Thursday evening, but in reality, we'd actually left in the middle of the night on Wednesday."

Well, I supposed that explained the meal, which appeared to have been staged. "I guess your mom's plan worked. Everyone does assume that the family disappeared on Thursday evening."

"Yes, it was a good diversion."

"But how did you get away? The family car was still in the garage, and I understand the family only owned one vehicle."

"My dad paid cash for an old van. He bought window shades so no one could see inside, and he parked it in the forest behind the house. We left through the rear gate. Dad put on a wig and hat, and he drove while the rest of us hid in the back. Once we got safely away from Washington, my dad dumped the van, and he paid cash for a station wagon that was being sold by a guy who didn't seem to care about legalities, and was just happy for the money."

"It sounds like your dad had a lot of cash."

"He did. It wasn't in the bank. He was a frugal sort of guy who stashed as much cash as he could in a lockbox he kept in a locked drawer."

"And after you left Gooseberry Bay?"

She sighed. "We drove around for weeks and weeks. Eventually, my mom was able to talk my dad into looking for a place to settle down. By this point, I'd had my birthday and was eighteen, so I told my parents I wanted my independence. They said that if I left the family, I had to cut all ties. I couldn't even know where they'd settled or what name they'd be living under. I didn't want to lose the people I loved most in the world, but I was just so tired of running that I agreed. I think watching them drive away that final time was the hardest thing I'd ever had to do."

"Wow," I said. "That must have been so hard. I can't even imagine."

"It was pretty awful."

"So, what did you do next?"

"I had a boyfriend, Logan Hudson. He'd lived in Gooseberry Bay for a while, but he moved to Seattle a year before my family left the area. We stayed in touch despite my father's rule about cutting all ties. He was a year older than I was and had his own apartment, so I called him and told him I was on my own, and he let me stay with him. Four years ago, we were married, and three years ago, we had Arial."

"Are you happy?" I asked.

"As happy as I can be. I love my husband and daughter, and I've never regretted making the decision I did, but I do miss my family, and I wonder what's become of them."

"You don't have any way of getting ahold of them?" I asked.

"No."

What an incredibly sad story. I supposed it was a better story than finding out that the family had been massacred, but barely. I wondered about the other children. Courtney had been thirteen five years ago, which meant she'd be eighteen now. I wondered if, like her older sister, she'd decide that the freedom of independence was worth the cost.

"Once we realized that Vanessa Hudson and Hannah Hamish were most likely the same person, we actually thought for a minute that you might have married Kyle Hudson," I said.

She grinned. "Kyle is a nice guy, and I did know him in high school. Kyle and Logan aren't related as far as I know, but I suppose Hudson is a fairly common name." She paused and seemed to be thinking about it. "If you were looking in the yearbook from my senior year, Logan wouldn't have been in it since he graduated a year ahead of me." After another brief pause, she continued. "Actually, I shouldn't have been in it either. I left in November, and I didn't take senior photos."

"It wasn't your senior photo we found, but a photo taken of a crowd, and you were standing in the background."

She laughed. "That is the exact sort of thing that would have sent my dad through the roof. If we'd still been here in Gooseberry Bay when the yearbook came out and he would have seen the photo, he would have had a fit."

"So I have to ask," I said after a few minutes of chitchat. "Why did you come up to me on the street that day? Given everything you've told me, it seems like sort of a big risk."

"I hadn't planned to. I'm not sure why I even did. Logan was out of town on a business trip, so I decided to take a short trip with Arial to see what was left of the fall colors. I hadn't planned to come to Gooseberry Bay. I was actually going to take the ferry across from Seattle and maybe try to find a place to stay on Bainbridge Island, but I ended up at the bay. I really only planned to drive through, and I wasn't going to stay even for a meal since I couldn't risk anyone recognizing me, but for some reason, I found myself driving by the old house. I was surprised to see that it was still empty."

"Yeah, we were surprised about that as well. I guess it's owned by someone named John Smith."

"I have no idea who that is. My dad never mentioned the name."

"So, you drove down the street and saw me at the house." I prompted.

"Yes," she answered. "I pulled the car around the corner and parked and then Arial and I walked back toward the house. I'm not sure why I stopped to talk to you. It makes no sense that I would. But I guess I was curious as to why you were at the house, and then you said you were working with Parker, and it occurred to me that you might be able to find out about the blue sedan."

"You wanted to know if it was real," I said. "You wanted to know if your dad had a real reason to flee, and that he'd made the right choice in doing so, or if his paranoia got to him, and he uprooted the family for no reason."

"Basically," she agreed. "I promised my family when I left that I would never try to find them, and at the time, that was a promise I planned to keep. But now I have Arial, and I want her to know her grandparents and her aunts. If the danger was real, and others had actually seen a blue sedan, and it seemed my dad had a real reason to move us, I'd leave it alone, but I feel like the bad men he believes he's being chased by only exist in his mind. Yes, ten years ago, he overheard something that he shouldn't have, and yes, it seems likely, especially given the fact that he was shot by an unidentified individual in a parking garage, that at the time, his life may have been in danger. But that has been so long ago, and as far as I can tell, no one followed us once we left Houston. I really think that the ten years my father has spent uprooting the family to escape the danger he is certain is lurking out there has been a waste. A waste of his life and a waste of all of our lives as well."

"Whatever happened to the man who killed his mistress?" I asked.

"As far as I know, he went to prison and is still there. Which is another reason that I don't necessarily think that anyone has spent the past ten years chasing after my dad."

"Yeah," I said. "I think you could be right. It does seem like the danger might be in your dad's mind rather than in reality." I paused. "Do you think you might try to find your family?"

"Maybe. Which is where you come in."

That's right. This conversation started with Vanessa saying that she thought I might be able to help her. "Okay. How can I help?"

"I haven't worked it all out yet. Courtney is eighteen now. I'm not even sure she's still with the rest of the family. She was always so independent and outgoing that I imagine she left as I did. I figure she would be the family member most likely to respond to me if I was able to track her down and ask for a meeting. The thing is, I have no idea where she is, or even who she is by this point."

"And you think we can help you figure that out?"

"Maybe. Parker is a really good reporter."

"I suppose there might be something we could come up with that would allow you to let Courtney know where you are or how to contact you. Do you think she suspects that you came back to the area after you left your family?"

"I do. She knew how much I loved Gooseberry Bay. She probably doesn't know I ended up in Seattle, but if I had to guess, she's most likely followed the news in Gooseberry Bay. She had friends here as well. Good friends that she cared about. After I left, I still read the online edition of the newspaper every week, which is how I knew about Parker. I won't be at all surprised to find out that Courtney has done the same thing."

"So, what is your real name?" I asked.

"Actually, it's Vanessa. After I left my family, I decided to reclaim Vanessa, or Nessa, as my family called me. Before marrying Logan, I also decided to reclaim my original last name, which is Bryant."

"And Courtney? What was her original name?" I asked.

"Jennifer, or Jen, to the family. Sarah is really Carolyn or Caro, and Laura is really Stephanie or Steph."

"So maybe we can figure out a way for Nessa to send a message to Jen in the newspaper. A message that Jen will understand if she sees it. Something with an email or a phone number she can use to get ahold of you should she choose to follow up."

"It couldn't be too obvious," she said. "But maybe the right sort of message would work. A message that's hidden in an ad, for example."

"Let me talk to Parker and the others," I said. "Maybe they'll have an idea about how to best do this. Why don't you call me back Friday afternoon? That will give me time to meet with everyone and come up with a plan."

"Okay. But remember, all of this is between us for now."

"I agree. They've agreed as well. You can trust Parker and the others. Yes, Parker wants to get a story out of this, but she's most concerned about keeping everyone safe. I'm certain she won't print anything you don't agree to."

Chapter 10

I couldn't believe how nervous I was as I drove toward Piney Point for my lunch with Adam. The last time I'd made the trip to the mansion on the bluff, Josie had been with me, and her chatter and light mood had somehow made things easier. Of course, this time, Kai and Kallie were with me, which was nice as well. I was anxious to meet Adam's dog, Hitchcock, and I was pretty sure Kai and Kallie would enjoy meeting him as well.

I thought about the man that I'd already formed so many different opinions about. When I'd first looked him up, I'd had an impression of a sophisticated man who was most likely boorish and entitled. He hadn't been smiling in any of the photos I'd pulled up, which made him seem so different from the smiling and easygoing guy I'd met at Hank's Hardware. And then there was the man who'd helped me rescue Damon. He'd endured personal injury in the form of long claw marks on his arm to make sure Damon was given the opportunity for a new home. I remembered how gentle he'd been. How he held the kitten close to his body and even managed to calm him despite the fact that just seconds earlier, the kitten had been totally freaking out. And then there was the man I'd had lunch with Tuesday. He'd been pleasant and polite. Professional. He'd listened intently to what I'd had to say, asked all the right questions, and yet for the majority of the meal, he hadn't seemed at all like the warm and friendly guy I'd run into up on the bluff. There was that one moment when we'd been talking about Mr. Johnson when I'd felt as if I'd been gifted with a glimpse of the open and tender heart behind the sophisticated exterior.

As we crossed the bridge that would take us to the road leading up to the estate, I struggled to calm my mind and focus on my breathing. The last thing I wanted to do was to show up totally freaked out before we even got started. Actually, the last thing I wanted to do was to have a nosebleed like I did the last time I'd visited the estate. I knew what to expect this time, and I felt like I had more control over my emotions. Adam seemed to want to help me find my answers. It made sense that I would let him. I just needed to be open and honest, and I needed to take things as they came, rather than trying to force an answer I wasn't sure that I even wanted.

I parked in front of the giant home and walked up the stairs to the huge front door. I rang the bell and waited. To be honest, I was expecting Ruth to answer.

She'd been the one to show us in when Josie and I had come to see Archie. I was pleasantly surprised when not only did Adam answer his own door, but he was dressed casually in jeans and a sweater, which made him appear a lot more approachable than he would have if he'd been wearing a suit or even slacks and a dress shirt.

"Ainsley." He smiled a warm and genuine smile. "I see you made it despite the rain that doesn't seem to be quite sure if it's finished or not."

"I heard the storm should blow through by the end of the day."

He looked toward my SUV. "Did you bring the dogs?"

I nodded. "I wanted to check out the situation before I let them out."

"Well, bring them in. Let's have a look at them."

I headed back to my SUV and opened the hatchback. Both dogs jumped out. After looking to me for permission to approach Adam, they trotted politely up to the front door to say hi. After Adam had greeted each dog, he called to his own, who I could hear pounding his way through the house, making it seem as if there was a whole herd of dogs running down the stairs rather than just one giant dog.

"Wow, he's gorgeous," I said as I waited for Hitchcock to greet Kai and Kallie before making his way over to me. "And so friendly and sweet."

"If he feels you to be a threat, he'll let you know in no uncertain terms that you might want to back off, but most of the time, he's a real sweetheart."

I ruffed the dog, who was even larger than my two, behind the ears, and then we all followed Adam up the stairs to the second story. When I'd been here with Josie, we hadn't gone upstairs, so I wasn't exactly sure what to expect. We traveled down a short hallway and then came to a doorway that opened into a large room with huge windows overlooking Gooseberry Bay.

"Wow," I said. "This is gorgeous." The room was an open floor plan that included a floor to ceiling fireplace, comfortable seating area, gourmet kitchen, and a dining area with a table I estimated might seat ten. A hallway was just beyond the kitchen, which Adam informed me led to a guest bathroom and three bedroom suites.

"This is my apartment within the larger home," he said. "When I'm home, I spend the majority of my time here. Archie has a mirror apartment in the wing on the other side of the house."

"This apartment is larger than the space most people raise a family in, and yet it feels tiny compared to the whole."

"Yes. It does seem that Bram Hemingway overdid things just a tad. This house more closely resembles the sort of huge estates you might find titled families owning in England, which I guess makes sense since Bram was born in London."

"This space within a space is perfect. It's warm and cozy, yet you have a lot of space to stretch out if you desire."

He motioned toward the table, which had already been set with crystal and china. "Ruth has prepared a simple meal for us. I thought we'd eat first and maybe get to know each other a bit, and then we can discuss your mystery."

"Sounds fine to me." I looked toward the living area and found all three dogs lying on thick rugs in front of the fire. They seemed happy and content, so I allowed Adam to help me into my chair.

"Ruth made us a pear and walnut salad, seafood chowder, and freshly baked bread," Adam said. "I hope you don't have any food allergies. I guess I should have thought to ask."

"No, I don't have any allergies. And the lunch Ruth prepared sounds wonderful. Do you normally eat up here in your own suite of rooms?"

"Sometimes. If Archie and I are both in town, Ruth tends to make a meal which we share with her and Moses downstairs in the kitchen. I guess you could say that Ruth and Moses are the closest thing to a family that Archie and I have, other than each other, of course."

"Do you spend time with your family overseas?" I asked after taking a sip of my iced tea.

"We do. Archie more often than me. They're good people, but they aren't our people if you know what I mean."

I nodded. "I think I do. When my dad was alive, he was my family in a way that no one else was. Now that he's gone, I guess I'll need to find a new family. Don't get me wrong. I have friends. Wonderful friends. But there's something different about having someone who really belongs to you."

"Exactly."

"I've enjoyed getting to know the gang out on the peninsula," I said as I dug into the wonderful-looking salad. "I'm not sure how long I'll be staying in the area, but for the time being, they are beginning to feel like a family of sorts. Especially Jemma and Josie. I can count on one hand the number of dinners I've had on my own since I've been here. If they're around, which they usually are, they make a point of inviting me over."

"I'm glad you're fitting in. The gang out on the peninsula is a special breed. They seem to truly care about each other and the community as well. Hope too," he added, "even though she doesn't actually live out there."

We spent the next twenty minutes eating the delicious meal Ruth had provided and getting to know each other. Once we'd finished, we moved into the center of the large great room where sofas framed the fireplace. Adam asked me about my research to date, and I filled him in on the few new details I'd picked up since we'd last spoken. I hadn't learned a lot, but I thought it was important that I'd figured out that my name had most likely been Ava when I'd stayed here a quarter of a century ago.

"That actually fits what I found," he said.

I sat forward. "Found? What did you find?"

"Don't get too excited." He smiled. "I'm afraid it isn't a lot, but after we spoke, I spent some time trying to figure out who might have been around in the summer of ninety-five. Archie and I both agree that neither of us was here during your visit, and we agree that our mother hadn't been, either. Mr. Johnson has passed on. Mrs. Adaline moved to Texas. Unfortunately, the last address and phone number I have for her are no longer good, and I haven't found any forwarding information. I can keep trying to find her, but it might take a while. I did manage to speak to Mrs. Rivers, and she reminded me that she went to England with us that summer, but she also reminded me that a young man named Timothy worked here at the estate helping Mr. Johnson during the gardening season. She'd kept in touch with Timothy, who was seventeen that summer, but is married and has children of his own now, so I called him, and he did remember two women who stayed here at the estate with two children for the majority of the summer."

"Did he know who we were or why we were here?"

"No. Well, sort of," he corrected. "Keep in mind that Timothy was a part-time outdoor helper who only worked during the height of the growing season. He was seventeen at the time, and not all that interested in two women who showed up with two children in tow, but he did remember that the blond-haired woman was named Marilee and the dark-haired woman was named Wilma. Timothy said that the blond-haired woman looked a lot like the two little girls. He thought she was an aunt and said the older of the two little girls called her Mame."

I supposed that was why I initially remembered calling her Mama even though she didn't feel like a mother. Mame wasn't all that different than Mama. "Did he remember the name of the two children?"

"Not at first, but I talked to him for a while to try to stoke his memory. Eventually, he remembered that the older of the two was named Ava. He never remembered the name Avery, but when I asked him if the baby might have been named Avery, he agreed that sounded right."

"Did he know why we were here?"

He shook his head. "No. He said he remembered the group showing up in early June, and he thinks they were gone by Labor Day. He worked out in the yard and probably never even went inside the house, but he did work with Mr. Johnson, who he remembered had been quite taken with you. I guess he talked about the cute things you said and did all the time."

"Aw. I knew I liked him."

"I know this isn't a lot since Timothy had no idea why you were here or where you went after you left. I figure what he did remember won't help much with the larger mystery you're trying to solve, but I will keep looking."

"Can you think of anyone else who might know something?"

"In addition to the staff who lived on the estate, there were a lot of part-time helpers. I remember the cleaning staff coming in most weekdays, and there were delivery people and the caterers who helped with parties and events. There is good reason to believe that someone who might have been more interested in two women with two children in tow than Timothy was might have stopped to chat with one of the women. Maybe they even asked a few questions."

I leaned back into the soft cushions of the sofa. "Thank you for everything. Really. I'm sure chasing down the details to my story has been time-consuming, and I know you're a very busy man."

"I don't mind helping if I can. I have to say that your story has intrigued me." He placed his hands on his knees. "My father kept an office on the third floor. I never go in there. As far as I know, Archie doesn't, either. I do know that he left files and files of documents behind. Most of it is related to business dealings, but he had shelves with photo albums and boxes of old letters and diaries. There are employee records as well. I can't promise I'll find anything, but I'm home for the next eight weeks, so I'll have some free time on my hands. I'd be willing to see what I can find."

"Thank you. That is so nice of you. I really appreciate it."

He shrugged. "As I said, I have some time on my hands. Once I go through and get things sorted, maybe you can come back by and help me look through everything a bit more closely."

"I'd be more than happy to. In fact, I'd really enjoy that." I paused and looked out the window. The rain had stopped, but the sky was still heavy with clouds. I'd heard the storm was supposed to blow through, and the sky should lighten, but I also knew that the weather didn't always cooperate. I was really enjoying my time with Adam, but I didn't want to end up driving home in a downpour.

"Did someone tell you about the Winter Ball?" he asked.

I turned away from the window and looked at him. "Josie mentioned it that day she came up here with me."

"It will be on the nineteenth this year. Archie is the one who organizes the whole thing, and I'm sure he'll think to send you an invite, but in the event that it slips his mind, I want you to know that you are invited."

I smiled. "Thank you. It sounds like fun."

"It's a bit Cinderella for my taste, but Archie is really into the elegance and romance of the whole thing, so I show up in tails and dance with all the eligible ladies in the land. Actually, I try to dance with all the ladies, eligible or not. It makes Archie happy, and I know that giving him exactly what he wants from me one night a year won't kill me."

"I take it the dancing you're referring to is of the ballroom variety."

"Yes. It's all very formal. Do you know how to dance?"

"No, not really. I mean, I've spent time in clubs where all I had to do was move my body to the sound of the music, but when it comes to anything more formal, I'm afraid I'll be lost."

"Don't worry. I'll teach you."

"You're going to give me ballroom dancing lessons?"

He shrugged. "I don't see why not. Archie will want you to be there, and you'll feel awkward if you don't at least know how to waltz. When you come by to look through the items in my father's office, we can practice."

I hated to admit how very good that sounded. Not only had I always wanted to learn ballroom dancing, but I imagined that waltzing around an empty ballroom with Adam would be magical.

"How long have you been holding the ball?" I asked.

Adam answered. "Before my parents died, they held a ball every year at Christmas. At least every year that I can remember. Then after they died, Archie and I decided that we really weren't into it, so we stopped hosting the balls. Then about five years ago, Archie met a woman whose attention he was determined to attract and announced that it seemed time that the House on Piney Point once again did its part for the community by decorating the way our mother used to and then holding the grandest ball in all the land."

I laughed. "Did it work? Did Archie get the girl?"

Adam shook his head. "I'm afraid not. The girl did come to the ball, where she met one of our cousins who lives overseas. They are very happily married and expecting their first child, a son, from what I've heard."

"Ouch. Poor Archie."

"Archie is fine. He really isn't the sort to settle down, and this particular girl definitely had settling down on her mind. But he did enjoy the ball. He seemed to enjoy decorating the house and planning the food as much as the event itself, so in a moment of weakness, I allowed him to convince me to swear that no matter what else was going on in our lives, the Winchester Brothers would always be together to do Christmas and the Winter Ball like they really should be done."

"I think that's a sweet story, and I, for one, can't wait to see all your decorations. I've never been to a ball, but it does sound magical."

"You'll need a dress. I doubt you will be able to get what you need here in Gooseberry Bay, so you might need to make a trip to Seattle."

"I can do that. I haven't been anywhere since I arrived. I'll see if Jemma and Josie want to come along. We can have a girl's day. If that doesn't work out, I'll order something online." I glanced out the window again. "I should get going. It looks like we might get another good dump before the storm blows through." I stood up. "Thank you again. And please call me if you find anything. And as far as helping with the stuff in your father's office and ballroom dancing lessons, anytime is great with me. You have my cell number. Just call or text."

"Okay. Give me a day or two, and then we'll set up a time to meet."

I looked at my two large dogs, who were sleeping next to Adam's large dog. "I think this was more of a sleep date than a play date. I don't think any of them have moved since they first settled in."

"Hitchcock sleeps a lot. I assume your dogs do as well."

"They do."

"They're great dogs. Feel free to bring them with you any time you stop by." He paused. "Well, maybe don't bring them to the ball, but any other time is fine."

"Okay. I will. And thanks again."

"I'll show you out."

After Adam walked me downstairs, he walked me out to my car. As I was pulling away, I noticed Ruth open the door. He walked over to where she was standing and kissed her on the cheek. It was sweet that he was so close to his employee. Out of the corner of my eye, I noticed Adam put an arm around Ruth's shoulder, and then the two of them walked into the house together.

Chapter 11

I'd called Parker about my conversation with Vanessa, and we decided to meet for dinner to come up with a plan to help Vanessa find her family. I wondered if Josie got tired of cooking for everyone almost every night, but I figured if she didn't want to continue, she could always say something.

"So, how was your lunch with Adam?" Josie asked before I even stepped into the cottage through the doorway.

"It was productive. I won't go so far as to say that I learned anything earth-shattering, but Adam did speak to an ex-employee who confirmed that two women stayed at the house during the summer of ninety-five. He also was able to find out the women were named Marilee and Wilma, and that the older of the two children was called Ava. He wasn't as sure about the baby, but when Adam fed him the name Avery, he said that sounded right."

"Well, that's something," Jemma said.

"It is something," I agreed. "Adam is going to look through documents his dad left in his office, and we're going to get together again. I really appreciate the number of hours he's putting into this thing. I know he's a busy man, so it means a lot that he's willing to dig into this. He could have just said that he doesn't remember meeting the women and children and leave it at that."

"I told you that Adam was a good guy."

"You did. Everyone did. I'm not sure why I didn't believe it. I guess I had this image in my mind of someone who was a bit of an elitist. But so far, Adam mostly seems pretty down to earth. Maybe not quite as down to earth as Archie is, but still a really nice guy."

"He is. And it sounds like your trip up to the bluff was worth your time."

"It was. Not only was I able to further confirm that I'd most likely spent several months at the house during that summer, but I managed to score an invite to the Winter Ball as well."

Jemma smiled. "It's a wonderful event. Josie and I have gone the past two years, and I'm sure we'll go again this year. We can all go together if you want."

"That sounds like a wonderful plan. I'm going to need a dress. I'm afraid I don't have anything even remotely appropriate to wear to an event like that."

"Maybe we can all go dress shopping together," Jemma said just as Josie walked in the door from work.

"Did I hear someone say dress shopping?" Josie asked, setting down two large grocery bags.

"Ainsley mentioned needing a dress for the Winter Ball, and I thought we could all go dress shopping. Maybe even make a weekend out of it."

"I love that idea," Josie grinned. "But the only weekend I have totally free before the ball is this weekend."

Jemma smiled at me. "I'm free this weekend. How about you?"

I hesitated, glancing toward Kai and Kallie. "I'm not sure about going anywhere for the entire weekend. I have Kai and Kallie to consider."

Josie shrugged. "We'll ask Tegan and Booker to watch the dogs and the kittens. If they don't have plans, I'm sure they'd be willing. Tegan loves animals."

"Okay," I said, picturing the perfect Cinderella dress. "If Tegan and Booker can watch the animals, I'm in."

"Tegan should be home," Josie said. "She left the bar and grill before I did, and I had to stop for groceries. I'll call her."

As it turned out, Tegan was thrilled to babysit the animals, so it looked like Josie, Jemma, and I were going to Seattle on the Saturday morning ferry.

We spent the next twenty minutes talking about dresses, and the type of dress we each hoped to find. Josie dug two dresses out of the back of her closet, so I could see what she'd worn the past two years. Jemma had been a bit more practical and had sold the dresses she figured she'd probably never wear again to a second-hand store, but she had photos to share. Just talking about the magical night caused me to feel a tingling of excitement I hadn't experienced in a very long time.

"Parker's on her way up the walk," Jemma said a short time later. "Based on the bags she's carrying, it looks like she brought Thai from that new place that just opened up down near the harbor."

"I've been wanting to try that place," Josie said. "I hear the food is really good and different from the food you can get at other places in town."

After we'd all served ourselves from the takeout containers, we settled around the dining table to discuss Vanessa's conversation with me. Since I'd already filled everyone in on the specifics relating to the reason the family felt the need to run in the first place, tonight's meeting had more to do with figuring out a way we might be able to help Vanessa reach out to her sister. I had to admit that with all the aliases in the mix, it was hard to decide how to refer to each player. Vanessa felt more like Vanessa than Hannah to me since I'd actually met the woman, so I suggested we all refer to the eldest sister as Vanessa. As for the second oldest sister, who was both Courtney and Jennifer, we decided on Jen.

"Okay, so Vanessa voluntarily cut ties with her family after she turned eighteen so she could set out on her own," Josie started us off. "In order for the family to agree to set her free, she had to promise to let them go and never attempt to find them. The problem is that after five years, she's beginning to regret that promise, especially since by this point, she's convinced that the danger her father has spent a decade running from is all in his mind."

"That about sums it up," I said.

"And she wants us to help her find her family," Parker confirmed.

I nodded. "She mostly hopes to make a connection with Courtney, who I guess we're referring to as Jen. She'd be eighteen by now, and Vanessa feels that, as she had, Jen will want her freedom. Vanessa said she wouldn't be surprised to find that she's already left the family and set out on her own."

"You mentioned when we spoke, that Jen might have wanted to maintain a connection with Gooseberry Bay as Vanessa had, so it's Vanessa's hope that we might be able to find Jen via the newspaper," Parker said.

"Exactly. I was thinking of something like an ad. Not a tiny classified ad, but maybe a quarter-page ad where the message has to do with something else like the upcoming Christmas Village, but there could be a hidden message letting Jen know to contact her sister, Nessa, at the phone number provided. Or maybe it would be better to use an email."

"What if we dress Vanessa up as an elf," Josie said. "We can take a promo photo for the Christmas Village. The main part of the ad can have information about the upcoming event: where it will be held, hours of operation, that sort of thing. Then at the bottom, there could be a message that says something about Elf Nessa is hoping her sister elves will contact her about exciting elf opportunities. We can then provide a way to contact her. I do think an email would be best."

"It does seem that Jen would recognize Vanessa if she sees the ad," I said. "And it sounds to me that the name Nessa was a family nickname that not everyone would know."

"This whole thing will only work if Jen actually does see the ad, and if she does, in fact, recognize Vanessa," Parker pointed out. "We also have to assume that she wants to get ahold of her sister and that she's in a situation where she can send an email. There are a lot of *ifs*, and I would say the likelihood of success is low, but providing a service announcement about the event is something the newspaper will do anyway, and as long as Vanessa is willing to pose for the photo, I don't see the harm in including her in the promo."

"Do you think others from Gooseberry Bay will recognize her as well?" Jemma asked. "Would showing up alive after everyone assumes she's probably dead bring more attention to her than she might want at this point?"

"Maybe," I agreed.

"Seems like including an actual photo of Vanessa might be too much of a risk," Jemma said.

"We could do it with random elves of a similar age and hair color to the real sisters," I said. "Maybe there could be four elves in the sleigh, and the text below the sleigh could say something about Gooseberry Bay's Christmas Village being a family event, and Elf Nessa is hoping her sister elves, Jen, Caro, and Steph, will join her for the holiday festivities this year."

Everyone agreed that should work. Parker said she could run the promo in next week's Thanksgiving issue, which would publish on Wednesday. We just needed to get Vanessa's okay to use the family names. Parker decided to set the promo up either way. If Vanessa wasn't on board with the idea, she'd run the promotion without the sentence having to do with the sister elves.

Once we got that figured out, the conversation turned to our own Thanksgiving plans. Jemma and Josie were planning to host a dinner for everyone living on the peninsula. Parker and Jackson planned to attend, and I asked about Noah, who they were happy to include as well. Hope had mentioned that she would be dining at the inn with her guests. I wondered what sort of plans Archie and Adam had. Perhaps I should have asked him when I was at the house today. Eating a meal with just the two of them in such a huge house felt lonely to me, although if I had to guess, Ruth and Moses would be invited as well. It really did seem that the four residents of the

Winchester Estate were as much a family as any family I'd ever met.

Chapter 12

Jemma had spent the previous day digging around into both the murder of the woman in Houston, which had been at the root of Vanessa's family drama in the first place, and the events surrounding the subsequent arrest of the boyfriend, and the eventual arrest of the man who actually killed her. After a full day of digging on Friday, she felt she had a lot of information to offer Vanessa. Jemma was initially going to explain everything over the phone, but since the three of us were going to Seattle anyway, we decided to ask Vanessa if she would meet us for lunch. She agreed.

"You said you have news," Vanessa said after the four of us had settled at our table and ordered.

"I do," Jemma said. "It took a lot of digging, so bear with me while I try to organize my research into some sort of coherent explanation."

"However you want and need to tell it is fine with me."

I had to admit that the poor thing looked nervous. I guess I would be as well. The events that had unfolded a decade ago had altered the lives of her entire family.

"The first thing I did was to identify the client your father had overheard speaking to the senior partner of the law firm. The client's name is Douglas Fairchild. As you described, he was a very powerful businessman with political aspirations. He started off by running for several local boards, but when all of this got started, he'd just announced that he'd put his hat in the ring for state senator." She looked directly at Vanessa. "As you indicated to Ainsley, Fairchild was an ambitious man with his eyes on the White House at some point down the road. He was married with three children when he found out that his much younger mistress was pregnant. When the woman was found dead, as you'd shared, her boyfriend was initially arrested. But, as you also shared, your father found a tape recording of the meeting he'd overheard, and he eventually sent that tape recording anonymously to a local reporter known for his hard-hitting exposés."

"Yes, that all sounds right," she said. "But other than the name of the killer, I already knew all of this. You said you had news."

Jemma nodded her head slightly. "Hang on, I'm getting there. The first thing I wanted to check out was the current whereabouts of both Douglas Fairchild and the attorney who helped him cover up the murder."

"And?" she asked.

"And both men are still in prison. Fairchild was charged with first-degree murder since it was determined that his shoving his mistress and her hitting her head wasn't what killed her, but the strangulation that came after. When you add the fact that the woman was pregnant to the mix, it appears that Fairchild will most likely never see the light of day."

"So, he couldn't be after my father."

Jemma shook her head. "He could not."

"And the attorney?" she asked.

"An in-depth investigation was conducted after the tape was released, and it was determined that Fairchild wasn't the only client this particular attorney had helped out in a less than legal manner. He was tried on multiple counts of wrong-doing, and while he may at some point get out of prison, he isn't out at this point, and hasn't been for the past ten years."

"So he isn't after my father, either," Vanessa said.

"Not personally. After I identified the two men who'd been involved in the tape-recorded meeting, I looked into the activity of the man who broke the story, newspaper reporter Lance Chariton. During the investigation and trial ten years ago, Lance had been asked to reveal the name of his source several times. Lance, however, insisted from the beginning that the tape had come to him with a note from an anonymous source, and he had no way of knowing who that source might have been. He used the information provided in the tape recording as a jumping-off point to prove what had actually happened. I can't find any mention of your dad at all. Not ever. Not in court records, arrest warrants, interview documents. Nowhere."

"But my dad was shot," Vanessa pointed out. "Someone must have known what he'd done and decided to get revenge of some sort."

"Yeah, about that," Jemma said. She took a sip of her water. "How long was it after your dad was shot that the family decided to pack up and leave?"

"Immediately after he got out of the hospital." She frowned. "It seems like he was shot on a Friday while walking through a parking garage after his day job. I think he was in the hospital for a week." She bit her lower lip. "It might have been less than a week. I really don't remember exactly. My dad was shot in the back, but the bullet didn't hit any organs, so once they patched him up, he was actually okay."

"And after he was released?" Jemma asked.

"He'd already talked to my mother about running. She was frightened and agreed. She got everything packed up and ready to go while Dad was still at the hospital. The day he got out, we piled into the van and never looked back."

"So you were already gone by the time the trial actually took place," Jemma confirmed.

"Yes, I think so. The newspaper guy had run the story and provided his proof, and the local politician had been arrested, but there hadn't been any sort of trial yet. I remember my mom telling me that we needed to hide Dad so that the bad man couldn't get him. My dad wasn't sure how anyone had been able to identify him, but the fact that he'd been shot proved that someone wanted him out of the way. I suppose the wannabee politician didn't want to risk my dad being pulled in as a witness."

Jemma put her hand over Vanessa's. She gave it a squeeze. "Here's the thing. I looked into the event surrounding your father's shooting and found that over the course of the next eight months, seven other people were shot in parking garages in the area as they walked to their vehicles after they got off work."

Vanessa frowned. "Seven others?"

Jemma nodded. "Four men and three women. All shot in the back, all shot in parking garages in the same general neighborhood where your father was shot, all shot on a Friday around five-thirty."

"So, what are you saying?"

"I'm saying that your father's shooting was part of a spree that took place over eight months. It had nothing to do with whatever was going on with your dad's boss or the client he'd tried to clean up for."

Her eyes went totally blank. "What? I don't understand."

"Your dad was the first of eight victims. The man who shot him was eventually found and arrested. His name was Walter Palmer, and he killed himself in his jail cell after he was captured. Your dad may not have even known about the other victims or Palmer. It sounds like your family fled before the second of the eight shootings even occurred. Based on what you told Ainsley, your family moved around a lot during that first year. It seems unlikely that your dad would have been on a spree killer's radar."

"So we ran for nothing? No one was ever after us? My dad being shot was just a random act by a random shooter?"

Jemma nodded.

"Oh, my God." She paled. 'I can't believe this. How could my dad go ten years and never put all this together?"

Jemma squeezed the hand she'd been holding. "I don't know. He was scared. He thought he knew what happened. He thought he knew who tried to kill him. And he had good reason to feel that way. You all moved so many times and changed your names so often that there was no way for anyone to notify him to let him know about the other victims or the man who shot them."

Vanessa took a long drink of her water. She took several deep breaths as if trying to gather her emotions. "So no one is after my dad? No one is after any of us?"

"No, I don't think so," Jemma said.

Vanessa looked like she might faint, but after a minute, she smiled. "My family is safe. We can be together. I can introduce them to Arial."

"Keep in mind that it might take a while for your dad to come around to the truth," I said. "He's spent the past ten years believing in an enemy that never really existed. It's not going to be easy to talk him out of that."

"No," she agreed. "But I sure as heck intend to try." She looked down at the proof of the ad Parker had given to us to show Vanessa. "Is it too late to change this?"

"I don't think so," Jemma said. "What did you have in mind?"

"I want to be in the photo. The elf in the back. I want my family to have no doubt in their minds that it really is me reaching out to them should they happen to see the ad, which I do understand, isn't a given."

"I'll call Parker," I offered. "If the change can be made, I'm sure she'll be willing to accommodate you."

Chapter 13

Thanksgiving Day dawned bright and sunny. Jemma and Josie had invited the dogs and me to come over early. Josie was making cinnamon rolls, which we planned to eat while watching the parade. Tegan, Booker, Coop, and Noah were coming by later for dinner. Josie said something about eating around five-thirty since Noah had to work until five.

Adam had called me yesterday and invited me to come back to his place to help him look through the piles of documents he'd sorted. He and Archie would be having dinner with Ruth and Moses today, so he suggested that I might want to come by tomorrow around lunchtime. He warned me that there was a lot to go through and that it would likely take several visits to weed through the documents in order to find something we both hoped might be important, but spending the day with Adam in his huge mausoleum of a house seemed to be the best way I could think of to pass the time.

Parker had been able to make the change to the ad, so it featured Vanessa. The newspaper had published yesterday, and now all any of us could do was wait and see if Vanessa received an email from one or more members of her family.

"I love all the decorations," Josie said as we watched marching bands, floats, and giant balloons on the screen.

"New York really is a magical place at Christmas," I said. "Have you ever been?"

"No," Josie answered. "But I'd love to go someday. The store windows alone would be enough to justify the cost of a plane ticket."

"If you do go, you'll have to be sure to see the Rockettes and visit Rockefeller Center," I said. "There are actually a lot of really great things to experience any time of the year, but at Christmas, the place is truly magical."

"Did you go and look at the lights and windows when you lived there?" Jemma asked.

I nodded. "I did. Keni and I made a real effort to take in as much of the holiday splendor as we could."

"Have you spoken to her recently?" Josie asked. "Your friend, Keni."

"I spoke to her a few days ago, but I plan to call her today." I glanced at the clock. "I'm sure she's planning to get together with some of the gang, so perhaps I should call her now."

"That might be a good idea," Josie agreed.

I got up and stepped out onto the deck. I pulled out my phone and was about to call Keni when I noticed I had an incoming call. "Vanessa?"

"Yes, it's me. I hope it isn't too early."

"No. It's fine. What's going on?"

"I just wanted to let you know that the ad worked. I got an email from Jen late last night."

I smiled. "That's wonderful."

"She's living in Akron, but she wants to come and visit as soon as she can work it out."

"Is she still with the rest of the family?" I wondered.

"No, but she knows where they are and how to reach them. Once she grilled me a bit to make sure I really was Nessa and not just someone who looked like her older sister, Jen let me explain everything to her. Of course, she was as shocked as I was, but also very, very happy. She's missed me as much as I've missed her and wants us to be a family again. She agreed with me that convincing Dad that he'd been running from windmills was going to be a tough sell, but she said that she's pretty sure that Mom will be open to hearing what you all found. She told me that everyone is tired of running, and she thinks that Mom is ready for it to be over once and for all."

I smiled. "That's wonderful. I'm so happy for you. For all of you."

"I'm so grateful to you. To all of you. To Jemma for spending so much time looking into things and to Parker for her willingness to play down her story to protect me. I'm thankful for you and Josie for being there for me. For the first time since Arial was born, I actually feel hopeful that she will grow up knowing her aunts and grandparents."

The fact that Vanessa was so happy did my heart good. I couldn't even imagine how the family was going to deal with the fact that they'd spent the past decade running from an enemy that never really existed. I supposed they'd find a way to deal with it. It certainly seemed that the family had been strong enough to deal with everything else that had been thrown in their direction.

I still wanted to call Keni, but I really wanted to share my news with Jemma and Josie, so I headed back into the house to fill them in.

By the time I'd gotten around to calling Keni, it was late in the evening, and the dogs and I had returned to our cottage. What a day it had been. Not only had we been able to resolve a really complicated mystery, but we'd been able to help reconnect a family as well. Once Tegan, Booker, and Coop arrived, we'd caught them up on everything that had happened. Everyone was in a wonderful mood and making plans to go to a tree farm on Saturday to pick out trees for the cottages before everything was picked over when Noah arrived. Noah had to work, but he hadn't seemed interested in the outing anyway, but Tegan, Booker, Josie, Jemma, Coop, and I were all free that day. I'd never gotten a tree from a farm before. Josie shared that the one we were heading to was a cut your own sort of deal, which sounded like a lot of fun. I had my research session and dance lesson with Adam tomorrow. Depending on how that went, maybe I'd ask him if he wanted to come along.

I was on my way to my bedroom to change into my pajamas before curling up with a book in front of the fire when I heard my phone ding indicating that I had a text. When I opened my message app, I found a text from an unlisted number. The text simply said: *Ava is dead. It is best to let her stay that way.*

USA Today best-selling author Kathi Daley lives in beautiful Lake Tahoe with her husband, Ken. When she isn't writing, she likes spending time hiking the miles of desolate trails surrounding her home. She has authored more than a hundred and fifty books in thirteen series. Find out more about her books at www.kathidaley.com

Made in the USA
Middletown, DE
06 November 2020